Robert Lukins lives in Melbourne and has worked as an art researcher and journalist. His writing has been published widely, including in *The Big Issue*, *Rolling Stone*, *Crikey*, *Broadsheet* and *Overland*. *The Everlasting Sunday* is his first novel.

ROBERT LUKINS

the everlasting sunday

UQP

First published 2018 by University of Queensland Press
PO Box 6042, St Lucia, Queensland 4067 Australia

www.uqp.com.au
uqp@uqp.uq.edu.au

Copyright © Robert Lukins 2018
The moral rights of the author have been asserted.

This book is copyright. Except for private study, research,
criticism or reviews, as permitted under the Copyright Act,
no part of this book may be reproduced, stored in a retrieval system,
or transmitted in any form or by any means without prior
written permission. Enquiries should be made to the publisher.

Cover design by Sandy Cull, gogoGingko
Cover image by Justin Paget/Getty Images
Author photo by Eve Wilson
Typeset in Adobe Caslon Pro 12.5/17.5 pt by Post Pre-press Group, Brisbane
Printed in Australia by McPherson's Printing Group

The University of Queensland Press is assisted by the Australian Government
through the Australia Council, its arts funding and advisory body.

ISBN
978 0 7022 6005 6 (pbk)
978 0 7022 6121 3 (ePDF)
978 0 7022 6122 0 (ePub)
978 0 7022 6123 7 (Kindle)

 A catalogue record for this
book is available from the
National Library of Australia

University of Queensland Press uses papers that are natural, renewable
and recyclable products made from wood grown in sustainable forests.
The logging and manufacturing processes conform to the environmental
regulations of the country of origin.

To Easy

December, 1962

ONE

There are things more miraculous than love. Given the right motivation common water may, for instance, turn itself to solid ice. In the first hours of a Boxing Day this wonder of the sky was spoiling the blanket of sleeping Britain while a boy and his uncle left a London home.

The uncle at his steering wheel, the boy attending to the windscreen's fog with his rag, they found a cautious route out of the dark city. Darting flakes and the road's new white were caught by headlights without commentary. The uncle kept at his wheel, the boy at his rag, and slowed by the greasy tarmac they arrived at the motorway just as daylight began to prove the magic of all that common water having become ice.

The uncle gave the boy a grim smile as their eye-lines crossed, the man's chin decorated with squares of bloodied toilet paper from his pre-dawn shave. The boy turned at the noise of his suitcase sliding about the back seat: through the rear window he saw the city effecting a cowardly retreat.

If this all had to happen, he thought, let it do so without

delay. A consoling strategy formed, that it would be wonderfully childish if he were able to endure the full journey without speaking a word.

'Will be slow-going,' the uncle said, squinting as he drove them towards the climbing sun.

It was two o'clock when an advertisement painted against a brick wall broke the news that they'd crossed a county line into Shropshire. It was then an hour of constricting slush roads before they made the beginnings of a small village, where the uncle abandoned his map. He discarded it to the boy, who made no greater sense of its yellow and black veins and lonely red-penned cross.

The uncle pointed – 'Here' – and mimed for the window to be lowered.

They jerked to a halt by a black church in whose shadow a woman pulled a trolley along the roadside. Her coat collar and headscarf conspired into a woven helmet and it took three impassioned *excuse me*s from the uncle to earn her attention. When she looked up at last to locate the source of her walk's interruption she revealed a face that was not nearly as aged as the boy had expected. Its apparent youth did not belong to a body making that kind of nasty angle with the ground. She stepped into the road and peered through the passenger window.

'Hello, excuse me,' the uncle said, craning forward. 'Sorry to trouble you.'

'No trouble,' she said with surprising brutality.

'Do you know Goodwin Manor? Could you direct us? Our instructions have left us short. And what with this weather. Quite remarkable. All this … well, snow.'

The woman narrowed with a new curiosity. 'The Manor?' She tilted closer and the boy sank deeper into his shoulders.

'That's right.' The uncle nodded his enthusiasm and a pink flake of tissue came unstuck from his upper lip. 'I hope we haven't strayed far.'

As if suddenly aware of the cold the woman drew herself into a hug. The youth that the boy had imagined in her disappeared into the vortex of her collapsing lips. 'For the house are you, lad?'

The uncle gently backhanded the boy, who kept his eyes to his lap and nodded.

'Are we within hope?' the uncle tried.

'You're close.'

'Fabulous. Great news.'

The boy grew aware of the woman's dauntless gaze at his temple.

'Go here.' She exhaled and indicated ahead to where the road broke off to the left. 'You shan't need to turn again. Up through the hills and you'll find it soon enough. Seven or eight miles, if that many. It keeps a distance from town. Not as far as it could, mind.'

The uncle offered a wave but it addressed only a fresh rush of snow, the woman having turned smartly back to her journey. Her serpentine shape had already returned to shadow as the boy wound up his window with what he considered to be admirably contained rage.

'Seven or eight miles,' the uncle said, taking the car into the mouth of the side road. 'Keep your eyes out.'

They ground on, the machine fighting the incline of rising land. Grazing fields on either side supported the occasional farmhouse or shed. Hills presented like frozen sea swells spotted with huddled animals.

He had heard of these beasts they called stock. Seemed an unnecessary joke, to call them stock while alive, then slaughter them, dry them, grind and cube them, only to call them stock again. He had also heard of sheep sitting and finding themselves stuck with ice to the ground. They had to be found and freed lest they never stood again. Did they fleece the unfortunate ones? Almost certainly. Did they wait for them to thaw? Perhaps not. Either way they completed that short round trip back to stock.

'Keep your eyes out,' the uncle would repeat each time they might have travelled a mile.

They were reduced to a slither as the road's edges vanished into banks of dirt. The uncle began to whistle a tune that was without melody or mercy while hedges ran close alongside, their barbed limbs slapping the paintwork.

The boy worked his rag at the windshield as vicious nature closed in. A horse reared and scattered a clump of pitch-nosed sheep. The car centred in its funnel until at once the bramble broke away and the road became a course of bends. Tyres skidded and the engine rose to a high whiz each time the uncle wrenched his wheel to change course. As he was thrown against the passenger door with reassuring violence, the boy's thoughts drifted to his dog in its warm city kennel. With each collision he overdrew this picture with a shade of envy. The dog's name was Barley, though the boy realised this mattered less and less with each conquered mile.

Back when the boy first learnt of where he was destined, he had imagined a world with a palette of only grasses – a sickly living green – but everything here was monochrome, divided between white and places in full mutiny against the sun. Despite the meadows with their low plants and creatures, this place had the comforting look of death.

Good grief, the boy thought, wondering if this kind of melodramatic reflection might become commonplace out here among the pastures.

In what could only have been pouting retaliation, signals of life came crowding into view as a final corner was turned and a slope's crest was breached. The boy saw the peaked maroon roofs of buildings. Smoke rejoiced from chimneys. A copse of amber trees gave way to a long brick wall and the opening of a driveway between two piers. A tarnished green sign hung in storybook fashion against the stone: *Goodwin Manor*.

The boy felt the beginnings of the joy that follows a long-denied arrival but soon remembered the sulk he had established over the course of the day. He let his arms refold across his chest as the car came into the entranceway and brought them to a pause. Ahead stood the awkward face of a great old house and before that a drive and perhaps a dozen human figures diffused across the hidden pebbles and lawn.

They were boys, all of them.

The nearer, strolling ones had turned their heads at the sound of the engine but had as quickly returned to their business of walking. Three were attending to a tree stump with their shovels while one leant beside against the handle of an axe. The largest group remained ahead, sitting on chairs and boxes near the high arch of the front door. A silver cloud of cigarette smoke hung above, caught in the frigid air.

'Right-oh,' the uncle said finally and drove them on.

The group by the door dissipated, moving into the house or meandering off with abruptly found purpose. Only one remained by the time the car came to its stop. He stood tall and ascetic, drawing hard on his cigarette and fixing his eyes on the passenger seat. As the car doors were opened this lone attendee dropped his stare, stubbed out against the brickwork and went off across the lawn. The boy exchanged an indeterminate look with his uncle, who rubbed his hands together excessively and jogged the long way around.

'Here,' he said, 'let's have your things,' and reached through to the back seat to retrieve the suitcase.

The snowfall had grown heavier and the boy watched shards piling up at his uncle's shoulders, into the thick burgundy of his hair. All was silent but for the heaving and swearing of the boys still working on the tree stump fifty yards away. The uncle shuffled until his toes met the boy's, motioned like it was the beginning of a hug, but baulked and gracelessly lowered the case to the ground. This action was the finishing of something, the boy realised. The completion of a transaction. The uncle inspected the grey sky, eyeing the source of all this cold and trouble.

'Looking bad,' he said.

The boy nodded.

'If I'm to be back home any time soon, any *day* ...' He puffed out his cheeks and blew, a misplaced gesture of summer. 'Worried about that motorway. If they can't clear the ice it's going to get itself closed. I've work on early.'

None of this was the fault of the uncle but the boy could not bring himself to ease the man's anxiety. It would be too kind, too close to a surrender.

'Seems like a decent place.' His uncle experimented with a smile. 'A good place for a while. The right place.'

They stood for five seconds more before the uncle reached some internal conclusion, squeezed the boy on his upper arm and skipped back to the driver's side. The car started and was aimed around in a messy series of turns before wheezing away. It came level with the workers and their tree stump, where the one with the axe had now taken the weapon into action. The remaining three laughed and passed around a lit match as the plum-cheeked logger attacked the ground. The car vanished beyond the end of the drive and its walls, the engine coughing somewhere on the other side.

Inside the house, he waited. Something would happen. Some sort of process would be enacted and a series of sensible actions would follow. He waited for what must have been fifteen minutes and not a thing transpired, not an innuendo of logic. Just a boy in a hallway with a suitcase and no clue what came next, so he began to explore.

Each room offered nothing more than indirect evidence of occupancy – dirtied plates, loaded ashtrays and the floor fresh with mud. Each time he heard the echo of a voice he would follow only to find it grow quiet and then silent, its owner burrowed somewhere deeper. He had circled back to the entrance and was considering how best to make his unease apparent when a head thrust itself around a corner.

This, and the rest that followed, belonged to a boy who filled the hall with a fair, nauseating energy. 'Your name is Radford?'

The arrival – *Radford* – nodded, relieved that he would not be forced outside to ask an opinion of the ruddy axeboy, yet resentful of this undisciplined decency, this demon sprite who smiled too broadly and was running his hands through his hair in a manner that reeked of secret knowledge.

'I'm West,' it said and turned away towards a narrow staircase that led into only more darkness. 'Come on, you'll be wanted upstairs.'

At this he bounded off – and truly bounded, like a keen foxhound might – and was soon out of sight. Radford followed, having to hold his suitcase at a peculiar angle to avoid the close walls.

A slim rectangle of window gave light as they stood in an antechamber before a closed door. The ceiling was too near and left the boys facing each other with a subtle stoop, their foreheads drawing together. Radford had to work hard to avoid engaging with West, who responded by increasing the width and intensity of his smile and inclining ever closer.

'West, as I said.' He outstretched his palm.

Radford submitted to shaking hands but leached any expression from his face that could be construed as recognition of their mutual existences. He made a show of brushing plaster dust from a corner of his case as the door was yanked open.

'Righty-oh?' asked the man who appeared.

'He has arrived,' West answered and gave an exaggerated hand roll.

'I see,' said the man as he pressed forward and stared gravely for some time.

Radford was taken by the hand. It was an act that seemed irregular, but having taken place, and showing no sign of being withdrawn, was accepted as some malicious convention. The man led him into the room, pushing the door closed as he went, speaking over his shoulder to West, giving instruction for him to wait with the suitcase.

They wouldn't be long.

The room was how a never-returned explorer's might be enshrined. Each inch of wall was overrun by shelved books, their spines forming a discordant wallpaper. Small tables were scattered about, crowded with papers, photo frames, river stones, pyramids of rolled maps and other accidental formations of unlike objects. Radford scanned for shrunken heads. At a glance he could see three vases of dead flowers.

They navigated around an oak writing desk obscured beneath precarious book stacks to facing chairs beneath the room's window. The man retained firm hold of him as they sat in the pillar of daylight. Snow pecked a faint noise against the glass while orbs of dust drifted between their two bodies. Radford examined the man's shoes, which were polished but scarred, exposed beneath trouser hems that had grown thin. The man's waistcoat was missing one button and the one that remained was broken, leaving just a half-moon to keep the fabric together. The jacket was pressed but shabby at the elbows and the knot of the man's tie was grazed on its face.

Outside, West squeaked against floorboards. Inside, Radford tried to remember the last time his hand had been held. Now the man added a second palm to the act such that he held both of Radford's. Having completed this ligature they resumed motionlessness.

Taking the tour of the man above the shirt collar he discovered a face that must have been fifty years old. Or sixty. This man, who maintained his stare, must be older than his uncle, which rendered him dangerously distant.

What part of this was test? Initiation. It could be the staring or equally the silence. This was where he was supposed to crack. The hand-holding was certainly part of the trial. Yes. How he broke this hold was to mark him a thug or a coward. So he would not break free and this faded turnkey could clutch him until kingdom came if he fancied.

Distantly, it seemed that West continued to find reason to scuff his shoes and, beyond that, music played. It could only be a taunt. Radford couldn't hear the tune but something about its beat declared it as a challenge before it disappeared as if a door somewhere had been closed. He returned to the man's face and they continued their duel of inaction.

Perhaps it was the shock of an older age in such proximity. Perhaps it was the meal he'd skipped. But all at once his seventeen years folded in on themselves and it was overwhelming. His breathing stuttered and he felt the man's grip tighten. This should have felt oppressive and Radford could still not recall being held in this way. He looked to the man and saw new detail. Wrinkles like shallow wounds marked the cheeks and brow. The hair was grey but not yet silver and it was a good head of hair. The nose had seen a lot of sun and survived. The eyes could have belonged to the dog back home.

'You're terribly lonely,' the man said, 'aren't you?'

Radford braced himself as his chest ceased its functions. The pair sat fully still for another minute that seemed to enclose a whole life and for all of it he did not breathe but began to tremble. The man did not move in blame or indulgence, merely allowing this and never relinquishing his grip. Radford could summon not a single sneering response. He thought, for that brief time, only of being exposed, of its companion terror, and of what it might be like to be safe.

Just as Radford caught hold of himself, the man gave a chummy pat on the wrist. 'Well, no need for that, there are plenty of us here,' he said and returned Radford's hand. 'You can stay if you like.'

'Yes.'

This had been the first word he had spoken that day and yet he felt no pride in this demonstration of resistance. Rather, his throat was sore from the effort. The man was standing and waiting, his expression acknowledging nothing of their exchange. On how many occasions had he made this same diagnosis of a boy, and did this lessen its legitimacy or confirm it? Once again there was music: that same unidentifiable song with its rhythm of squeaking soles.

'Yes, coming,' Radford said, rubbing his shirt sleeve across his nose and rising, hurrying after the man, who had moved with haste to the door.

'My name is Edward Wilson,' the man said, 'but the boys will insist on calling me Teddy. You call me whatever you like. Not sir, not Wilson.'

Radford gathered himself and the door was opened to expose West, first standing at attention then tossing his head to one side expectantly.

'Find the boy a room, will you, he'll be staying.'

'He could pile in with Lewis,' West said.

'Oh no. Heaven, not that.' Teddy raised his eyes to the ceiling. 'Give him Rich's quarters.'

'And Rich?'

Teddy made irritated motions for the pair to get away. 'Move him to the chickens' coop. He won't be expecting that.'

West gave a performative salute as Teddy turned away and closed himself behind the door.

'The others will be envious,' West said, lifting the suitcase. 'Rich's room is a good one. Far from the toilet. View of the pond.'

Radford considered their earlier meeting and felt a flicker of embarrassment. 'Hello,' he said, striking out his hand in belated greeting if not reparation. 'I'm Radford.'

'Well, yes,' West said and gripped the case hard to his chest as if it were a football. He launched downwards, whooping, and Radford – having retracted his hand from its pathetic error – ran after.

The house was no pretender of authority. It gave no effort to an impression of being an asylum, a prison or any amalgam of the two. It seemed, if anything, to have been fashioned from the innards of innumerable aunts' drawing rooms, all rugs on rugs and browns on browns, the wallpaper generations thick. Radford had followed West into a hallway with chambers running both sides and heads projecting suddenly from doorways. As West brought them to the end he towed a crowd jostling to inspect the foundling.

'His name is Radford,' West announced as they poured into a room. 'We must make space. Where's Rich?'

'Gone to the village,' said a long, freckled face. 'He and Lewis think they've got a chance with the bakery girl.'

'Well, he's been sent down to the chicken house.' There was some dark laughter at this. 'It's a luckless day. The least we can do is set him up well in his new digs.'

Bodies continued to maraud in, sallow figures scoffing and competing, and in small time the room had been stripped. The vandalism seemed practised and the vacating tribe left only a bare bed and a wardrobe with its doors swung open to reveal vacant hangers. Someone pushed an armful of trousers into Radford's arms and he was pulled into the hall and absorbed into the running huddle, a half-dozen, now sunny as they charged downwards, the plundered loot of Rich's room aloft. There had been no time to form a defence; Radford was centred in the pack as West started to *cluck* and *bekirk* at the front. The others copied and, having rampaged a dining room and kitchen, they were disgorged to continue their exercise across the snow.

'Keep up, little one.' West slugged Radford on the back, and he hugged Rich's trousers tighter still, stumbling ever colder.

They made the rear of the building and over his shoulder Radford saw the full scale of its confused shape. It was as if a village had coalesced over time into a single structure. What might once have been stables and servants' quarters, family cottages, had been drawn in with the central house. Walls and pitched roofs of different centuries met at both strange and obvious angles like the grafted limbs he had seen on his grandparents' roses.

The freckled boy slipped and came down hard, spilling his cargo. Others slowed to observe the accident and poked around at the fallen goods until someone ahead shouted something accusatory and they regained their pace, crowing as one. It was unclear how much of this was brotherly and how much unkind. The snowfall was coming for Radford as he strained to keep straight, finding himself alongside a short figure with Roman, serious features. This boy nodded as introduction, adjusting his blankets to shake hands and, looking satisfied, promptly vanished.

As they rounded the building's far end a frail wooden shed came into view and a coven of chickens scattered. The coop.

Radford felt unease at the sight of it. His arrival was forcing this unmet Rich to be put up in the fowls' house and it was simultaneously too daft and too severe. He had expected this place to be a situation close to purgatory, yet here they were in the midst of an infant school's jape. He wanted to return to sleep, to its persistent past.

Hay bales were dragged in, brushed clean of their snowy caps and ordered into the shape of furniture. One of these, waist-high and wrapped in sheets, became a bed. A wooden crate on its end resembled a bedside table. More hay was amassed against a wall, creating nooks into which clothes were affectionately folded and made into bundles, and around all this chickens returned, pecking and curious at their new ornaments.

Radford neatened his armful of trousers into a pile and found a home for them. The coop offered toy resistance to the weather's enterprise and when the wind turned parallel it delivered a gush of fresh ice. The boys shivered and their chatter dulled. West made attempts to pull the leaning door closed but it scraped and stopped solid against the muck. He had come through carrying an archaic lantern and, with two others lifting him by the belt, hung it over an exposed nail in a roof beam.

'A palace.' West dusted off his hands as his toes touched earth. 'Rich can only be delighted.'

Gazes were dodged as another nasty gust blew through the walls and rattled the tin. One boy motioned to leave and the rest departed as an undisciplined company, West making himself last, trying again but with less effort to bring the door shut. The others ran back at the big house, with no more clucking or congratulation. Radford and West cantered in tow, each folding arms against their torsos.

'This Rich will really be sent out?'

'Of course,' West said.

Reaching the same patch of blanched earth that had claimed the freckled boy, Radford lost his feet and was only just caught by the shoulder.

'Teddy will have his little edicts,' West said, righting him. 'They're only to keep the game alive, nothing to be frightened of.'

It would be admitting too much, to respond. Radford was the first of the pair inside and he chased the sounds of warring life back to the upstairs hall. West followed and failed twice to have them speak, halting at the entrance to Radford's room as he lifted his suitcase to the mattress. Radford evacuated its clothes, holding them for a time at the yawning mouth of the wardrobe before thinking better and placing the stack on the floor. The case went under the bed and Radford on top, shuffling until he sat with his back flat to the wall.

'Feeding's around six,' West said. 'I'll knock when it's up.' He allowed time for acknowledgement to remain unspoken and pulled the door closed.

Radford stayed straight, refusing the temptation to lie down. Half an hour it had taken for simplicity to have been poisoned. Even the bareness of his new room was false, an absence instead of an emptiness. This was not as he had intended. There had been the purest of plans, to be silent and dumb. Then came Teddy and West with their complicating kindness. Those two had intruded so quickly and completely, and Rich, whoever he turned out to be, was now to live out in a slurry of snow and guano for no reason other than Radford's presence. This Rich would hate him for it and so in turn would the rest.

The hanging bare bulb glowed yellow. How useless, as unremarkable darkness lay behind and ahead. On the opposite wall the plaster's age grew in a branching fissure until it butted up against more recent material. The door too was modern with rough gaps remaining around its frame and it occurred to Radford that his room had been created by splitting a larger in two. He stopped himself only a second before turning this inconsiderable fact of architecture into metaphor. Enough, enough of all this. Enough cleverness. The seams of his arrival had been torn but his ultimate plan was untouchable. All that remained was to see it out, to not have it distracted.

Weariness descended and he removed his shoes.

Across was a window that may well have looked down at a pond, but from Radford's position he could see only cloud ready to drop its storm.

The Manor was a place for boys who had been found by trouble. Those were the words the man from the government had used: *found by trouble*. He had been addressing Radford's mother and in that instant the boy had wanted more than anything to be able to injure time, to go back and remove what it had witnessed; to unstitch this ill that had found him.

The government man explained that the house was by a long shot the best option they would be offered. The alternative was a more difficult place. He had called on favours and twisted the arms of several important people to have the Manor be even a possibility. Radford and his mother, it was explained, did not realise how fortunate they had been. The Manor was something they must be grateful for.

When the knock came Radford was by the glass. Outside, just the meringue peaks of landscape were visible by the light from ground-floor windows.

'Housekeeping.' West came in whistling and dropped a pillow and blankets. His buoyancy must have been that of driftwood. It could not be a living thing.

'Thank you.'

'Supper will be up,' West said. 'You're coming?'

As they travelled others joined, some starting on tussles that ended in only messed hair and threats. An approximately handsome figure came upon Radford, inspecting him and all the while sharpening the point of his quiff. He asked questions and West answered Radford's name and presented him as a pet might be introduced to a household of children.

'And this is Brass,' West said, biting his thumb. 'Ignore any and every thing he has to say. His is a mind unencumbered by reason.'

'You mustn't blame our West for his little digs,' Brass said. 'He gets his frustrations all confused with his jealousies. And he has an awful lot of frustrations.'

They moved ever downwards.

'You're *society*?' Brass asked. 'Come clean if you are, it's no crime.'

Radford felt his mother's steamy breath on his neck. He briefly pondered how answering this could do anything but confirm the false accusation. West threw his hands up in objection.

'Jesus, sensitive,' Brass said, forfeiting his interest and starting again on his hair.

They arrived in the dining room, where four long tables made rows by mismatched lounges and kitchen chairs. An upright piano and a radio sat in a corner and the fireplace took up the far wall's centre. Twenty or thirty boys were already roaming in noisy clans, all gripping food bowls and making huffy declarations to the warmth. West called Radford into the kitchen and handed him a dish and spoon. From one of the two copper pots steaming beside a cube of bread rolls he claimed a serve of the fair-looking stew.

Back in the dining room West's lot took over a table's end and Brass shared around jam jars filled with a murky foam. West clutched his and took a swig. It took two attempts for Radford to recognise the sour-bread aroma of beer. Brass was watching, egging on with conspiratorial eyebrows.

'Get stuck in, will you?' he said. 'Before it's seen.'

Radford wrapped his hands around the glass. By virtue of being West's discovery he had been brought among this subset. The ease of this was why it could not be trusted. Nonetheless he lifted the beer to his lips and let it pour in. Bitterness muddled with wood turning to ash; all the world became the inside of a football boot. He thought of his uncle filling his sitting room with the scent of burnt sugar and oil while cleaning engine parts.

The one named Lewis arrived flustered. He ploughed his meal while working himself into an indignant lather over the actions of an aggressor he never quite named. He had been put offside with the cook, blamed in absentia for some crime with the potatoes, and his protestations had been so great that they were taken as an admission. He went on, raging ever hotter until he spotted the beer and his words ran loudly together. West clamped his mouth and drew him into a clinch, slashing a finger at his throat. Lewis nodded, his eyes growing wide as Brass produced a tall open bottle from between his feet and halved its contents.

Radford watched the alcohol take. Smiles were begun and extinguished, the beer and stew settled and as minutes succeeded they all grew slow and contented. Circumscribing Radford, they spoke and joked easily. They were a mongrel outfit, accents and skins from all over, some looking separated by at least a few years.

Brass jostled like he might be the eldest, perhaps as old as nineteen. His hair, on which he performed constant maintenance, was oiled into a greaser style. His cheeks were drawn with pink perforations yet the pallid, scarred skin somehow amplified his glamour, giving it a defiant narration.

Lewis was the tallest in the room, his head peaked with a ragged blonde outcrop. He sat with a stoop, which only emphasised his length; his broomstick arms waved around in wide, wind-making signals.

West: still wildly keen, ever contriving circumstances in which to be generous.

Radford considered adopting shame at the anger that had run through him. He had felt such fury at West, at being wrong-footed so quickly, but now not a spark of offence remained. West's face cycled through expressions of devotion; it seeming to have no normal, never finding a state of rest.

Another boy came crashing down, all bother and its redness. He was as short as Lewis was long. They made sympathetic bookends, matching each other's gestures as they began to fight over, then forget, then change subjects in the space of single breaths. Dark rings were drawn around his eyes and his lips were white and dry. He looked ill, like he never slept.

'What is this about the chicken coop?' he demanded, as if suddenly giving birth to consciousness. So this was Rich.

West took to explaining the matter of his relocation and made a thin call for compassion against the laughter that had come after. It was a directive from the chief, he offered. Rich reminded them of the certainty of his imminent death, which was countered with an assurance of the coop's new tasteful décor.

Rich buried his face in the tabletop, though he shook enough of his sullenness to blindly reach over and command Radford's hand into a shake. 'You're staying?'

At this Radford diverted his eyes in apology and glanced at West.

'His won't be the only life you'll ruin, I assure you.' Brass looked to Radford and laughed into his froth. 'Dicky's demise is a burden you will learn to live with.'

Radford drank and attempted a smile and begged his poisoning blood to lead his mind to sweet places. He retreated into the fog of where cold met fire. All started up about him, mostly laughter, mostly at Rich's expense. The story was told of the day in the village and of Lewis's chance with the baker's girl, Frances, being foiled by Rich's secondary advance. The facts were disputed but it seemed that in a moment of panicked bravado Rich had attempted a verse of 'It's Now or Never'. Lewis insisted that he and Frances shared a rare connection. Rich maintained that his serenade had been justified. Regardless, the baker had emerged floured and cross, ordering his daughter into the back of the shop and the boys into the street. Frances's concession to either boy's tactic remained unrecorded.

'Rough.' Brass pulled fingers through the hair at his temples. 'Even I wouldn't try Elvis.'

'No, Rich, it was very brave of you.' West began to cluck and flap his elbows, with the rest joining in, crowing and scratching at the table.

It went on and Radford succumbed to the medley of voices and their uncomplicated rhythm. He had been ignored, the truest acceptance. A chilling wind came through the room and some made closer for the fire, which in return scattered its flames and sparked protest. The corner of a burning log pulsed between bright and dull and as it did Radford allowed his muscles to finally relax. He could not believe evening had come. In this place time seemed unanchored to the wider world. The house floated within reality as an island and he was merely one of those dumped to its beach by storm. Home, now, he supposed. A drive and a suitcase was all it had taken: how slippery the idea had been all along. What else lay waiting, pretending to permanence? The beer was turning thick in his veins and sending signals for slumber. The chatter circled and weaved a cocoon.

'Boy.'

Sleep called.

After everything, it could all be okay.

'Radford.'

It was West's hands that shook him back to sentience, to Teddy standing expectant at the room's entrance. The man wore a dressing-gown with a pipe peeking from its breast pocket.

'The house has made welcome?' Teddy asked, gesturing with the appliance and speaking so all could hear.

Radford nodded, minutely, already wishing this away.

'I wonder if they have mentioned the entertainment, the celebration of your first evening. That some show is made. All silly of course, but it has become a tradition.'

The room turned to Radford and he wondered if the effect was that intended. The horrid, terrorising attention. This was a man who hours ago had taken his hands and so precisely punctured his caul, but here he was, wounding with all these eyes.

'So, no-one has told you.' Teddy's face gave nothing away.

Simply, this was not fair. Radford felt his cognition reduce to that of a toddler. After the kindness he'd been shown, this was *not fair*.

He infused a lone syllable, 'No,' with all the furious import he could muster.

'We are in luck.' Teddy was addressing all the others. 'Radford is something of a sensation at the piano.'

He had considered himself safe for a time, now this treachery, and he wondered how Teddy had invented the ammunition. He imagined his mother hunched over paperwork at their kitchen table, angered and tearful, profiling her son and becoming stumped at *Hobbies and Interests*. He looked to those near for a cue but Brass wouldn't meet his eye and Rich nodded as if this was to be expected.

Radford tensed. 'I don't know what you mean me to say.'

'You'll give us a tune?'

So this place was to be no different. Unseen, Teddy must have made gestures for Radford to be seized and dragged to the piano, for a rash of boys leapt to their feet and did just that. Pulled across the room, his wrists throttled together, feet held from the floor, he could only marvel at the ingenuity of this torture. He could have been beaten or had a balloon of urine emptied over him as he slept. This was something else.

He was lowered to the stool and had to throw his hands out to stop from cannoning into the instrument and in doing so struck the keys and brought a clap of untuned thunder. There was a weak cheer. Having spent years below ground, the recollection of his first football match surfaced. Malcolm Allison had put it into the back of the net with five minutes to go and he had never heard a noise like it. A roar, but like dinosaurs had made. Back then it had shaken him and he had cried with the excitement. He had been put onto a stranger's shoulders and punched at the sky.

Teddy waved for the concert to proceed and something not as grand as a hush spread through the hall. Some near the back sat up on a table. West's lot stood on chairs, West himself a fool with both fists clenched and held above his head. Every one, traitors all. If this was to be a humiliation, he would make it a great one. A dumb energy brewed in Radford and radiated to his limbs. Hands into balls, he raised them, the knuckles just touching.

He made a commitment: he would expose nothing of himself to this house.

The fists came down and the noise was fabulous. Chords bent into shapes that had never existed. No right note would come from Radford and his chest shook with the volume and anarchy. It felt too, too good. Better than knifing pillows or putting an elbow through a bathroom wall. Better than spearing a fencepost through any number of parked cars' windows. He went on, vaulting across the keyboard.

Looking back he saw, among the considerable apathy, a few gentle smiles. In patches, pleasure. In a space between fist-falls was a whoop of encouragement: it was West, commanding. Brass sucked two fingers and whistled while Rich jammed out his wings and crowed the proud rooster. Teddy remained silent but wafted his pipe like some weary conductor.

Radford brought down his hands in a concluding gesture and the final disassembly of notes rang out. They failed to be consumed by a roar of delinquent approval but neither did they echo alone. Having pushed away the stool he came back through the room and was neglected and blessed in equal measure. At his table he was dragged into a huddle. Teddy, warlord or no, left clapping sympathetically, and the riddle remained of what any of it meant.

'Tradition,' West announced and upended the dregs of beer into Radford's hair.

*

They conquered the staircase as secretively as five teenagers might.

After the turn on the piano the room had resumed a regular hum and Radford had settled on listening to the near voices. For their part the others never mentioned his recital. The failures with Frances sustained conversation. The first night in the coop still lay ahead for Rich and this wasn't permitted to be forgotten, fowl impersonation coming without restraint, Lewis taking particular delight and swelling with luxury at each instance.

As diversion it was Rich who first mentioned cigarettes. Pockets were pulled out empty and a melancholy fell over them.

The taste of beer was fading from Radford's tongue and he was lamenting this when he found it composing the surprise: 'I've got some.' The others had stirred as a family of dogs around dropped ham. 'I've a pouch,' Radford went on. 'Anyone have papers?'

Lewis showed a fistful of rolling sheets and so it was that they were running, running not at all secretively upstairs. They went to Radford's room, where he summoned the pouch from a roll of clothes, and as they didn't ask he didn't describe its theft from his uncle. They contrived to stay hidden from the house lest they be swamped with demand. They moved as a phalanx, Radford at its rear, and it was just as he brushed his hand on the stairs' top banister that he collided against a sudden wall. It was a boy, though the size of a grievous man, standing over him. The rogue monument stuck out a redeeming hand, its face bearing an uncertain smile of menace or worry.

'I'm sorry,' Radford said.

This seemed to bring some pain to the hulk, who said, 'That was a terrible song,' with a voice adult and controlled. It took a rise of the boy's great eyebrow for the insincerity to register with Radford.

'Oh, right. Yes, I had hoped so.'

'I'm Foster.'

The others came rambling back down the unlit hall and Radford was pushed aside. Brass took the titanic boy by the collar and Lewis grabbed for an arm. They got him back two steps, then came more censure and shoving and they were around this Foster in a half-wheel. They ordered retreat and he said nothing.

Radford objected, though without force. They had misunderstood Foster's intentions, yet he welcomed their bravery in his defence.

West arrived and got himself inside the confusion. 'Leave it,' he said, rocking onto his toes.

Foster looked limply to him, darkening.

'It's nothing,' Radford tried.

'Is it?' Brass turned ugly and to Foster. 'Are you nothing?'

Foster, without any kind of movement, accepted this, making no gesture of defiance. He could have smashed Brass to mince; instead he shrugged and went. West called out after him, 'We're having a smoke.'

'Jesus,' Brass protested. 'Not on your life.'

Foster didn't slow and as he rounded the corner his face held no malice. Radford said nothing and when the sound of boots had trailed off Rich shook a fist at the stairwell.

'Right,' Brass said as he checked his fringe. 'Now you've gone tough.'

'I helped.' Rich looked about for endorsement. 'I was there.'

'It was nothing,' Radford said again. West responded with a signal of futility.

'I thought we were civilised folk having a smoke,' Brass said and started them walking again.

West put his hand to Radford's shoulder as the others regained enthusiasm, beginning into a run, and Radford allowed himself to be taken by the shirt sleeve. He had abandoned the unknown Foster for the temptation of these unknown others. Darkness again, behind and ahead. He would get what he deserved.

'Matches, anyone?' came a voice, singing from above.

They came to rest beneath a square of night that went on forever. They had scaled stairs at the far end of the building and pushed out a fragile door to a stone-brick space with nothing above. It had boasted a roof and ceiling a hundred years previously, West explained, both long since gone. It was such a small room, and a needlessly inconvenient one, that through all the Manor's years of repair and renovation it had never graduated to the top of any list. The boys sat on its floor with their backs to the granite, their feet pointing in and touching at the centre.

'Was a belfry,' West said, pointing to the open cathedral arches of each wall. 'Bell would have hung right here. God knows why.' He mimed the pulling of a rope and began to lick the open edge of his cigarette.

A paper came to Radford via Rich, who was accused of ruthless capitalism after suggesting he could be paid back later. The truth of the cold's severity descended, and there was talk of whether the Ruskies had it right, of the redistribution of common property and where this left the very concept of First Division football. The shag separated itself between them.

They sat unprotected amid the snow but as none of the others showed worry then neither did Radford. He would feign trust at this, that something would come to dull the sting just as earlier the beer had arrived and taken them to a softer world. Others spoke without hesitation as they assembled their smokes. The air, brittle and still, became overwhelmed by tobacco. It was glorious and of the old earth, smelling of fertile ground disturbed by animals.

During one of several concurrent arguments between Rich and all the others, something was described as having taken place two years earlier. The question of how long Radford would be staying had never fully crossed his mind, but to speak of years was mad and impossible.

'Two years ago?' he interrupted.

The others smiled, all to different degrees and with various intents, and Radford sensed more pity and understanding than he could stomach. Talk turned to the wheat field Rich had set fire to the previous summer. He claimed no knowledge and offered no excuse for his loss of eyebrow. He was stockpiling cigarettes in his lap, rolling and rolling without ignition. The rest, with Radford, shared two matches and together smoked their share. They drew deeply, religiously.

'What's the point then?' Radford said, without being sure of what he was asking.

Brass tossed the book of matches. 'Who promised you a point?'

Lewis clapped for attention and pulled a folded blanket out from under him.

'Brilliant,' Rich said, granting all forgiveness.

Radford was certain he would never know these boys beyond surface – not their sources, or where they might be headed, and nothing could change this. Lewis cast out the blanket as a bait net and it rippled across their feet. A final offering went around and soon all was silent. Their cigs went ember-tipped and shivering chests held their blessed air. Radford tilted his head back against the stone. The burn was immediate through his hair but he wanted to investigate the sky, to see if it offered any greater wisdom.

His thoughts were shrinking in the cold. He should not be there. There was no reason for it. How on earth would it work? All heaven was dark.

Fragments of snow were falling on their blanket, catching in the low light and shining as the absent stars they stood in place of. It descended on their ruined belfry, a room pointless well before it was useless. Radford tried to think of his dog and where it was right then, how it would be finding satisfaction, but he had already lost the clear memory of it. It had not even been a day and the animal had become a canine stencil.

He pulled hard on his cigarette. The pilfering of the pouch had been a hasty, unplanned action, having presented itself in his uncle's kitchen the night before. Now it meant everything. He looked at these boys and wondered what each of them was keeping underneath. None had asked how he had come to be sent to the Manor. He drew back as he tilted again to the sky and released his plume towards that forever. Forever could handle it. Perhaps the others had no inner lives to speak of. Perhaps the others were shells too.

The fall grew heavier and the sky no less empty or infinite. The walls, even with their four vacant windows, gave the impression that one was at the bottom of a drained well. All was fallen in and trivial. Those shrivelled thoughts again.

'Bloody freezing,' someone said.

Everyone agreed.

Winter took no rest, proud with its beginnings.

Surveying the rooftops, where the old land met that of the humans, it found these young ones sitting huddled and unprotected. They made endless noise, becoming quiet only to tend to their smoking sticks. They made that birdcall they named laughter.

These creatures' mission seemed a selfish one. They were a destructive breed, so intent on bringing things to an end. So be it. Left alone, perhaps they would complete the dirty work themselves.

Winter would leave its judgement for now, for the clock of the moon ticked on and it had much to do.

Of course he would suicide.

The Manor was too much like something of a *Boy's Own* story. All too Tom Brown and the neat perils of boarding school. Perhaps Foster would play the thick-necked bully and there would be a dastardly teacher to make unstuck. All too cute.

It was some hours after midnight and Radford had returned alone to the belfry. The cold was now unbearable and the view plain black. He removed his shirt. Through the window space he could see nothing of this country, nothing of the iced fields and their shivering cattle.

In this place, this childish story, it would be the most childish act. He had grown accustomed to the thought of the word, suicide, aware it held power for some. It was a thing committed. Like fraud, like adultery. He took pride that he wouldn't resort to adult euphemism: there would be no ending it all, no topping of one's self. There was a perfectly serviceable word for it and it was one with all the right sounds. That hiss of a final exhalation.

He could escape from the house and walk into the lunar world and its death, but could he trust that it would take care of him, that some instinct would not take hold and find him shelter? It was the kind of betrayal he would recognise. He could find the kitchen and lay his head in the oven, but would that be, again, all too cute? They might not even be connected to the gas; he would need to check.

How dull that his story would end so soon and here. That flopping himself over the edge of some abyss would be the closest he came to theatre. That he could find no antagonist greater than himself.

Dreary, really.

His limbs and chest had pushed through burning into numbness, and that double-crossing agent, intuition, had sunk one of his hands into his trouser pocket and wrapped its finger about something. An unspent match. Visions of the Manor's caricature boys came to him and the feel of Teddy's warm, callused hands.

A primitive grunt came from the doorway. He turned.

'Heard you leave your room,' West said. He took the discarded shirt from the ground and pushed it into Radford's hands, coming to his side. 'Just came to be sure.' He connected their gazes. 'Do you mind?'

This silly boy, whom he knew so little of.

The cold became all at once too much and it hurt so greatly. Tears came in great convulsions and he leant into West as if he were the only thing able to keep his body from dissolving a star-shape through the stone floor.

West, for his part, simply stood.

Radford wept and all the salt water that proved him real fell across his face on its way to West's coat sleeve. When the time came West brought them back indoors and they parted in the hall as Radford came to his room. He closed the door quietly on West's still half-smiling face. He replaced his shirt and fixed its buttons.

TWO

The morning of New Year's Eve had been passing uneventfully until its cancellation. Radford had been attempting to split firewood with Rich when word came that the calendar was to be usurped. Teddy believed that it would be not at all right to celebrate the renewal of anything while the undignified weather persisted. The following morning was thus, for the second time in as many, the beginning of the year's final day. Subtly kinder falls had arrived through the night and so over breakfast Teddy decreed that as long as the weather held, so too would the date.

Radford was learning the ineffectiveness of pondering the internal argument of the house – what it governed and how it ruled. It was the new eve and that was that.

He had to concede it had already been more agreeable than the last, which had seen an unpleasant fight in the afternoon, between Lewis and one called Harris. Harris was small, one of the slightest in the house, so it had surprised everyone when he shoved Lewis hard from behind and started mouthing off. He spat that Lewis was a *lanky dolt*, *pathetic*, and that had been enough for Lewis to make a proper mess of his face. Any irreversible damage was only held off by a gang-tackle to the floor. One sat on Lewis's chest while another used knees to pin his arms to the boards. Harris was dragged away to the kitchen, blood hastening down his chin, and Rich took custody of Lewis. Radford followed them upstairs, holding Lewis's flat cap, which had spun under a table in the melee. They stopped at the midpoint of the hall, all regaining some composure. As it was pushed joylessly into the wall, Lewis's unprotected head made a rewarding *thunk*.

'Give up, will you?' Rich asked without menace.

The pair let their breath return and Lewis submitted to being straightened. Rich pulled at the neck of his jumper, righting it and evening its sleeves. He backtracked to Lewis's hair and proceeded to groom him down to his shoes. It was a delicate display and Radford watched on, anxious of how untroubled they were by his presence. The alliance between these two would seem brotherly if not for their willingness to succumb to it. A red trickle began from Lewis's nose.

Radford held out the cap and in a neat motion Rich took it and placed it on Lewis. 'You'll get sent down,' Rich said. 'And then we're shafted.'

'He called me pathetic.'

'You are.'

Lewis looked over Rich's shoulder. 'What's your take?'

'I have no opinion,' Radford said. 'And I'm not being polite. I don't know what on earth is happening.'

Blood ran freely into the deep crest of Lewis's smile.

After breakfast Brass took Radford to the kitchen to start into the dishes.

'Who are we?' asked the woman greeting their entrance. She held out a broad knife, having paused from halving vegetables, and seemed a ghost.

'Radford, this is Lilly.'

'Miss Grange,' she said warmly, tabling the tool and giving Radford her hand.

'Nice to meet you, Miss Grange.'

'Ooh, manners. Did you hear that?'

Brass started wiping with a tired-looking rag and grunted.

'Do you remember your first words to me? Do you?'

He gave a whimper.

'*Piss off*,' she said in a mouse's high pitch. 'Little charmer.'

'I had reason for it. And besides, since then,' Brass turned smart, 'Lilly and I have formed a bond. A close one. Lilly, would we call it inseparable?'

'Insufferable, maybe. But you,' she said, pointing between Radford's eyes, 'you, I love.' She pulled a cigarette from the pocket of her apron. 'Manners. You English make a lot of noise of being mannered, but it is only noise.' With this last line her accent dipped rashly somewhere near French.

Brass removed his jacket. 'Lilly, you're from Kent.'

The knife was spun on its point and left to fall back to the board.

'Ah, oui.' She flung herself against the counter and clutched both hands to her chest. 'But my 'eart will be-long always to my beloved city of Pair-ee. Oh, tell moi you believe.'

Brass shrugged into his suds. Radford wanted to give this woman all she wanted. To bring colour to her transparency.

'Of course,' Radford said. 'Oui.'

'A good'n,' she announced with a decidedly un-Continental burr. 'Let us drop this *Miss Grange*. Lillian. You will call me Lillian.'

'You won't recognise the honour,' Brass said as he spat into the water. 'There's a strictly enforced system at play.'

The woman bent forward with her smoke between her teeth, igniting it in the flame of the cooker's ring.

'Starts with *Miss Grange*,' Brass said. 'Then, if fortune smiles, you call her *Lillian* – though a feller doesn't usually get there in a week, so count your blessings – then if you're a tidy egg you call her *Lilly*, but only when you and her are proper little peas in a pod.'

She gave Brass an excessive, doting smile. 'I despise you.'

At this she floated behind him, the tips of her shoes touching his heels, and reached around to bring her cigarette to his lips. She held it in place just long enough for him to take a lingering drag. All the while his hands remained plunged beneath the surface of dirty bubbles.

Radford saw the sheen of Brass's rough charm, lit as it was by Lillian's affection. He was a twit, no doubt, but an arresting one. Radford stared into the bend of his neck, the way it welcomed the tufts of dark hair curling into its ears and the scratch of Lillian's fingernails.

It was a mother's insatiable love, wanting to eat her baby up.

By experiencing Brass as she did perhaps he could learn some of this power. He could develop a character. So he took Brass to be intoxicating, and saw him as beautiful.

'Good to have you,' Lillian said, stepping away and putting a hand to Radford's shoulder.

He nodded conspicuously and started at the breakfast bowls. As the three of them worked he listened to Lillian murmur and at times break into gentle song under her breath. She was all things. Her manner was that of one who had endured trials while her peach cheeks, her blonde bob, spoke of more bountiful times. She was, maybe, thirty-five. He imagined that she had once been softer or weaker and that something had tempered her, making her as he found her now, all strength and grace.

Almost a week had turned over: each day had brought not a sense of understanding but an understanding not to search for sense. When he asked how things operated in the Manor – timetables, lessons, chores, responsibilities – he would be met with reluctant, ponderous answers or more often none at all. No rules, only customs. A conscious vagueness inhabited the place whereby time was a thing to be occupied: an enemy's pillbox on a battlefield.

He asked what people did.

What do you mean?

The question seemed reasonable, pressing even, and it was unsettling that he had to probe for a response.

As in, what do we actually do, *all day?*

Oh, I don't know. There're always things to do.

This was the nearest to a solution he would find and he had accepted its certainty. There just were, always, things to do. Repairs, most often. The Manor was in a persistent state of decay and the boys worked against this, without hope of conclusion. In Radford's first days there had been a concerted effort to correct a particularly sagging beam in the dining hall: the labourers had seemed proud of the result but Radford noted that all but a few avoided walking beneath it.

There was no schooling, but things like lessons. Equivalents to teachers travelled out for the day, but others, Radford was warned, would stay for weeks or months at a time. He had come across some of this incohesive lot: a rose-skinned woman who taught the importance of accounting and the grim reality of ledgers; a bland young man in a hairy suit and bowtie who skipped about the Manor finding candidates for his dining-room tutorials on ancient and recent world history; and a stiff, brown farmer named Gall, who arrived from the neighbouring property, complaining on a tractor. With his shotgun over a shoulder, he took a reluctant troop out into the extremes to show them the right and only way to *hog a hedge*.

Even this day, the resurrected New Year's Eve, lessons were starting up about the house. Radford was preparing to return to his room when Teddy came through, slashing emphasis with his pipe and announcing that a *Manny* was to be giving thoughts on the art of electronics in the Long East Room. Radford reached the foot of the stairs exactly as Brass was likewise making an escape and they managed to wedge each other between the handrails. Brass was the first to break away, vaulting up three stairs at a time.

Teddy leant into the newel post and shouted after him.

'What brand of influence are you, child? One for greater or lesser?' He turned immaterially to Radford, who waited to be encumbered with the idea of this Manny's forum, but Teddy left, silent.

Was he not worthy of Teddy's guilt-giving?

Radford would of course have to attend, burdened as he now was with spite. He arrived in the Long East Room, to a man and wires. Everything about this figure assembling equipment at the room's head was wholly, unrepentantly *Manny*. Two inches shorter than average, his hair six inches longer. He was overweight but in an unremarkable way and his eyes were dark to a degree that robbed them of intrigue. Radford went around Teddy, who had swept ahead into the room, and took a chair against the wall.

The instructor was speaking too softly to hear, addressing no-one in particular as he put together boxes, jars and cabled tools. Five other unfamiliar boys occupied the room. They looked towards Teddy as if their presence was the paying of some penance.

Manny coughed loudly, seeming to startle himself. 'We are going to fix, that is, I'm going to show you the fixing of a radio.' He patted the top of a blue leathered box and peeked up, giving a flash of stained teeth.

'Keep the awful thing,' Teddy said. 'Stopped the week I bought it. Cost a packet. Bloody mess, actually.'

'Was there a smell?' Manny leant forward, inhaling, and Teddy took the opportunity to signal for the boys to move in closer. Chairs were dragged across the floor and drew Manny's attention to the tight oval suddenly surrounding him.

'Yes, a smell. Awful. Leave you to it.' Teddy departed with an abstract lunge of his pipe.

Manny unlatched the back of the radio and let it swing open, showing its insides of coloured strands intertwined to a maroon board. Metallic objects protruded in the shape of swollen safety pins, others like cotton reels or gleaming thimbles, and underlining this was a shaft sheathed in tightly wound copper.

'Roberts RT1,' he said, tapping the thing with a finger. 'Made out in Surrey. Their first all-transistor. Not the first in Britain, of course, that was the PAM 710. RT1 was later, '58. Then others. RT7, RT8. Yes, here's the thing.' Radford stretched to see the man unclip a blue and red block and drop it to the table. 'Nine volts. Not good, certainly not right. Should be just the six.' He put his finger to a label and read aloud. *'Very important – do not attempt to reverse battery leads or use a battery of other than six volts as damage to the transistors may result.'*

One of the boys nodded as if into sleep in the exact moment that two others pushed away from their chairs and left the room. Radford just caught Manny's intake of breath.

'Ah … but that's nine?' Radford asked.

'Yes.' The man corrected his fringe. 'Yes. Nine will blow a transistor. Less touchy than a valve, but they'll still blow. A week or a year, but it will go.'

One of the audience certainly yawned and another was absent in the view out the window, twisting knots into his shoulder-length hair. Manny began to rush through a canvas bag to produce another blue and red brick and a celebratory sigh.

'Six volts,' he said, gesturing with the battery at Radford. 'Attach that.'

With the slab in one hand Radford took hold of a stray wire and was about to push it against a protruding battery terminal when Manny barked. Radford checked the uninterested near faces and moved his wire towards the alternate terminal. He pushed the stud in, at which point Manny became animated and stole the works, beginning at the knobs. The radio gave a loud belch of static.

'The blown transistor needs discovering,' Manny said. 'We take our screwdriver and we give each a little tap.' He held the tip of the screwdriver to his nose and gave the gentlest of knocks, then exposed the box's circuitry. 'Just a tap.'

Tap.

Tap.

Radford strained, listening for something useful through the harsh buzz.

Tap.

Tap.

Tap – and a faraway human voice was given to life.

'... the hot sticky weather has done nothing to deter enormous Melbourne crowds from witnessing the battle of attrition that is this tense second Test ...'

Manny was all dusky smile, Radford too, until the newsreader's voice sank back into the wash. In the time it took Manny to find the replacement transistor the other boys were back attending at their window or mining back-teeth with thumbnails. Radford watched the man's movements with increasing consideration: the way he held the jars to the light and somehow gleaned enough identifying information of the components from the shapes and lengths and colours. They meant something, made contact. Manny extracted the broken part like a thoughtful dentist, remorsefully. Things were unscrewed, pliered, peered at and melted in place.

This soldering was the real magic.

Clouds blew out in explosive puffs as the point of the hot iron touched lead. The smell was sweet and potent and lingered as he twisted the radio's top dial and the machine again found reason to speak. A song filled the room, loud and strange, smuggled to earth in the falling snow. It had flooded the room as effectively as water and Radford imagined himself suspended. What a creature Manny was, what an odd and gentle wizard: the barrier separating him from the admiration of the other boys now seemed something precious.

Radford knew the feebleness of all this symbolism, yet as the solder fumes fell away his eyes met Manny's and something as secret and real as electricity was uncovered. The radio announcer took over.

'… *and that was The Shadows with their single, "Wonderful Land"*…'

'Fixed,' Manny announced, switching the radio dumb.

'Five minutes.'

Radford hid his arms from the wind. 'You've said that.'

'Just be ready.' West pointed a finger. 'I'll come get you. Where's your better coat?'

'Under my bed. Why do I need another coat?'

West put a hand to Radford's shoulder and gave a squeeze that provided no reassurance, then turned straight into Teddy, knocking them both halfway to the ground. After a deal of huffing and slapping away of hands they were upright again and West resumed his run towards the house.

'I am a frail old man,' Teddy insisted.

'He's gone,' Radford said after a time and pointed to the dirty expanse of snow between them and the kitchen door.

Pink with exertion, Teddy brushed again at his sleeves and pulled down on his jacket, assessing its straightness. He checked the knot of his tie.

'What is happening in five minutes?'

'No idea,' Radford replied truthfully, realising that they were now walking.

Teddy was perpetually walking, always to some place, never from, pulling whoever was near into the task.

'How are you finding things?'

'Fine,' Radford said.

'No, you're not.'

They continued past the far corner, by the coop. Through the gap between its doors Radford glimpsed Rich on his hay-bale bed wrapped to the chin in blankets and puffing gleefully on a cigarette.

'No,' Radford agreed.

'I'd worry if you were. Frankly, I'm surprised each morning when I head down for breakfast to discover that none of you have been murdered in your sleep. No need to look at me like that. I can't control what some profoundly disturbed child does with every minute of its day. I've toyed with the thought of putting locks on the doors but it might give the impression of a philosophy.'

'I don't know what you mean.'

'Guiding principles. The funders are forever pushing for them. It would make life easier for them in their meetings but I will tell you what I tell them all, that I endeavour only to keep you alive.'

'That's all?'

'That's a lot.'

Radford felt the back of his collar pulled and they came to a halt.

'Look,' Teddy commanded.

They had reached the far end of the grounds, where the dark wall marking the property's boundary had in places deteriorated to nothing. Neglect had punched through the stones. Through these great uneven gaps the view of endless, diamond fields rolled away.

The storm had kept the household bound indoors. The coop and the firewood stack were the furthest Radford had ventured and that had been in a bowed rush against the frightful cold. He was acquainted with the walls of the dining hall, the ceiling of his bedroom and that sooty infinity above the belfry. He knew the brown slush circling the entrance to the kitchen.

This view was of a novel world, crushing in its brilliance.

Country glistened and the pair stepped into a V-shaped space made by the wall's absent stone, Teddy gesturing. 'Our plot stops at the second hedgerow.' Zigzags drew territories into the distance. 'All would have been part of the Manor, once.' He found his pipe. 'The family owned well beyond what we can see. Neighbour Gall has the surrounding fields now and we let him put his sheep in to graze. Good man, from good people. Been farming here since well before I arrived.'

Radford lounged in the sunlight falling on his cheek. 'When was that?'

'The winter of '31. A real mess. The house had been left for twenty years and wasn't fit for its rats. That helped a little, I'm sure, when the Manor was put forward as a place to send lads. Particular lads. Couldn't be too agreeable an alternative.' He smiled from a mouth of pleasantly bankrupt teeth. 'We paused during the war, of course. Place was taken back as a convalescence hospital. Kept a few boys on, as many as I could squirrel away. Did them good to see men in that state.' Teddy examined the stem of his pipe and squinted back into the faraway. 'They sent me the file on you,' he said. 'Before you arrived. Everything. Everything that's happened.'

Radford looked to the near meadow, where some unconvincing goalposts set a football pitch apart. So it was all written, all put into words that would never leave him.

'I didn't read it,' Teddy said, rubbing his neck as if sore. 'Fed the fire with it like the others.'

Beyond them were a series of overlapping hills, iced smooth and diminishing into a haze. Radford felt his fibres slacken, his heart ease. A natural colonnade formed a line behind the small dot of a farmhouse.

'Do you know of the Royal Oak?' Teddy extended a finger towards a tall tree standing alone at the crest of a mound. 'The Oak? Charles II and the great escape?'

Radford shook his head.

'Oh, ready yourself. It is a time before now – I know the year but I won't tell you – and King Charles has just been defeated at the Battle of Worcester. He's on the run, Cromwell's armies chasing across England, and the promise of death hangs over anyone found to have given Charles protection. The King and his company travel by night. A royalist – by the name of Will Careless, if you can believe it – gives them shelter, but as the troops close in he knows the family house is unsafe and has Charles hide in the field's great oak. Later, Commonwealth troops stand directly beneath, sheltering, discussing their search – the King silently listening in. The coast clears and Charles continues his escape, smuggled to France and returning years later to retake the throne. For two centuries – I read this, so it could be true – Charles's birthday was celebrated by the wearing of a sprig of oak on the lapel. The tree that hid the King became the Royal Oak.'

Radford stared at the tree. It truly was remarkable, full and so strong. Limbs outstretched like a protector's arms though now holding only ice and birds. A small fleet of the creatures launched from its branches in an act that was indecently picturesque and suspiciously timed.

'Wonderful,' he said.

'Isn't it?'

He remained, allowing himself to be enthralled by the spidery silhouette.

'Of course, that isn't it,' Teddy said, still pointing. 'Not the Royal Oak. No, that's just a tree in a field.'

Radford considered a show of bright anger but found

ultimately against it. It could do nothing but make certain that all was as untrustworthy as it promised. He expanded his chest to allow room for the fury while, ahead, the birds returned to their resting place. It was obvious they had solved all the riddles of life. They had evolved in a direction away from these crippling piffles. They had only the moment-to-moment brawl for existence, the cheats.

'The Royal Oak's fifty miles away,' Teddy continued. 'Rochester. Though even that's not the real thing. That was ruined by tourists, damn shame. Lopped off the branches as souvenirs. The one on show is the Son of Royal Oak, or some such thing. Shame. Proper mess.'

Radford turned away from their distant, ordinary tree. 'I don't understand you at all.'

Teddy looked indiscreetly pleased.

On cue West arrived at their side. 'Christ, found you,' he said breathlessly.

'Trouble?' Teddy asked.

'Just bringing Radford his fleece. Absurd him being out here single-coated.'

'I have nothing to fear?'

West shouted benign satire after Teddy, who had about-faced and was already ten yards away. West waited until the man was out of sight before unveiling two bottles of bronze liquor. 'We've got somewhere to be.'

He cast the coat over Radford's face and ran them through the wall's gap as the sun eased around an expanse of cloud. The world beyond the Manor grew several shades brighter. Rich moved in front of them, hunched and running like a man under fire. Then Brass. They were sniggering and running in criss-crossed lines as Lewis loped through the snow with a blanket over his head, clutching another bottle.

Radford tired and asked of the destination.

'A wake.'

'Whose?'

West clinked the bottles together dangerously. 'Not sure, yet.'

They took the hills, falling into a military rhythm as they went. West kept himself at the front as if he were leading and Radford gave up on thought and followed, knowing he could at least apprehend the route of footprints. Confusing the way, Rich's trail writhed ahead, running side to side as he and Lewis made snowballs. They slackened but still found amusement in lobbing the occasional bomb of hail ahead, nailing West at least twice in the back of the head. The air, beyond chill, made short work of cutting through Radford's trousers and long johns. His socks became wet and winter made house in his bones.

Following a hedgerow that became a tall thicket at a valley's floor, they rounded a corner and a river of green glass came into view, twenty yards across at its narrowest point. It was a mirror threatening with honesty; snow pushed right to the edge, leaving a dark cuff of soil for the last few inches. Radford had known only the Thames and when that slowed to reflect its city it could never stay a clear picture. Always a pre-emptive blur of motion.

Brass barked against the silence and the troop gathered at the armless trunk of a downed tree.

'Pass, pass,' he said and the bottles went around.

'No.' Rich knitted himself. 'We wait 'til we get there. We always wait.'

'Christ's sake.' Brass brought an uncorked bottle to his face, squinted through the mouthful and let out a pained, operatic *aah*. 'This is proper rank.'

Rich replied with a clown's gesture.

'He has a little man in the village,' West said, tapping Radford. 'Fixes us up.'

'Top shelf.' Rich examined his bottle and had a secret sniff. 'Real deal.'

Radford took his turn and had to summon all his will to keep from ejecting it across the unready ground. His breath kept the smell of petrol and old flowers. In time the pain, though, turned to warmth and ran the length of his body, pooling in his boots.

'Well, I'm waiting 'til we're there,' Rich insisted, retucking his arms and walking ahead along the bank.

They corked and fell in behind.

From high above, where fates were decided, these boys appeared as helpless as they truly were. Winter's show was so great and rare it too could only wonder at what it was getting away with. These lonely humans here, these children, were like currants to be pressed into the cake's surface.

Winter explored its creation, in every direction white,

flying on its arrows through the spaces in trees and animals. The molecules of the air grew slow, longing to dance no more. Blood and sap tightened. Now would be the time for charity, for the granting of hope, but these were the same prideful mortals that took pleasure from defeating Winter so mercilessly. They were so quick with their fire and salt and showed no regret. These boys imagining themselves conquering miles, they pushed only deeper into the trap. Winter wondered who would miss them and how long it would take for others to follow with their shovels. Yes, it could bury them now and perhaps that would be the form charity would take, putting an end to their troubles.

Or it could have these boys prove themselves. Their own people saw them as errors. What would these children make of the true cold – would they still think it something to be corrected?

Winter would watch on for now. There was no risk of missing its chance, for Winter always returned.

Radford had been eyeing the flight of a curious bird that had escorted them the last hundred yards. It would skit back and forth, inches above their heads, landing in the crook of a branch or beside a slushy pool. The field flattened and the bird flew ahead, perching at last on a dark headstone that rose from the snow. A cemetery materialised.

Rich strode over the knee-high fence. It was solemnly rusted and missing in several places and Radford followed over its hopeless spikes. The others became animated at the arrival. Snowballs flew once again and applause rose as Rich failed to resist one down the back of his jacket.

'Always me,' he said, shaking the ice free. 'So predictable.'

Brass lit a cigarette and offered it. Rich looked on dubiously, but accepted it and made sounds of hardened thanks as another was lit and matches passed. Walking around a leaning cross, only fairly sure he was between the graves, Radford waited for someone to explain. No headstone remained true, with all fallen or on their way to it, and made more derelict by the clean snow.

'What are we doing?'

'A wake,' West said, lowering the bottle into Radford's hands. 'Like we said.'

West scamped along the row and bent himself to the inscriptions, straining at their scratched letters. Ahead, Lewis called out.

'Fanny Glenacre?'

'Done her.'

'Norman, ah. Norman Green?'

'Done.'

'Richard Pecker?'

Lewis and Rich faced one another, unsure.

'Yes, done the chap,' Brass said drearily through his cloud. 'Lewis called him Dick Pecker. It was a riot, I'm surprised you've forgotten.'

'Abraham Butcher,' West said. 'We haven't done Butcher.' He waited for confirmation, the others shrugged, so he rubbed hard at the stone. *'Abraham Butcher. Asleep. May the 2nd, 1856.'* He uncorked and looked into the distance as if in a pantomime. 'Abraham,' he started, redirecting his gaze downwards and shaking his head solemnly.

Radford cursed and stalked back through their footsteps. They could keep their wake and its private joke and he would give not one ounce of a damn. As he reached the fence his haste managed to snag his trouser. Yanking against what must have been the only stable section of the miserable relic he was sent facewards into the drift. Laughter sprang from behind him, joined by the crunch of footfalls. Hands lifted him upright and it was West, brushing his chest.

'Don't take offence. It's a game.'

'I'm not offended.' Radford pulled again at his ankle and the fabric tore with a gratifying rip. 'I just want plain speaking.'

'I'm sorry, look.' West flung his arms out, crucifying himself against the air. 'It's just a silly game and you're part of it, not the butt.'

Radford let his brow fall into slow acquiescence and they returned to the group.

'It's an act of kindness.' West took his place at the top of a rounded headstone, his boot heels dangling against its inscribed face. 'These poor devils are left out here alone. All unremembered, forgotten.'

'So we drink.' Brass raised his bottle.

'We commemorate,' West corrected. 'We celebrate and in doing so we remember them.' He addressed Radford again. 'We tell the plain stories of plain people, gone untold for too long. Abraham Butcher, as Rich was about to remind us, was an honourable man.'

Rich peered fretfully skywards, rubbing his upper arms. 'We should go back,' he said. 'It's turning.'

There was the moaning of unsympathetic cattle.

'Jesus, okay,' Rich said. 'Abraham Butcher was ... well, a great man.'

An ovation of screeches and saluting. West imitated a horn. Brass held three cigarettes between his lips.

'A courageous man,' Rich continued. 'Though modest, of course. Take his exploits at the battle of ... the battle of ...'

Radford was visited by a slideshow: the motorway drive with his uncle, the humiliation of the piano, Teddy's false Oak, the game these boys held out of reach. Impulse had tapped the juice of Radford's anger too easily. He would remember that his defence lay in retreat and he would deny himself to all others but when he deemed it profitable. He would show himself now, all so his absence could be more keenly known.

'Patootie Ridge,' Radford said, finishing Rich's thought.

Small laughter sent eavesdropping birds into flight. Rich waved his hand to signal that the floor was on offer.

'The battle of Patootie Ridge,' Radford affirmed.

'Which war, remind me?'

He spoke in a full and strange voice. 'The Boer,' Radford said. 'The second of the Boer Wars. He'd been dead for, what, forty years by that point? Precisely why his exploits were just so remarkable. And worth remembering.'

The audience raised their drink.

'He'd been on the sauce too,' Radford said. 'That's a fact so few realise about Abraham's actions that day. Hot as hell in Africa, especially for a Midlands man. Couldn't start the day without a gin and tonic and on this particular one he'd dealt with the best of his platoon's share before the sun rose to forty-five degrees. Proper elephant's trunk he was and that's probably why he was brandishing all three of those rifles and wearing two helmets when he led the unexpected first charge over the peak.'

Even Rich was applauding now between glances into the murderous sky. Brass lost all pretence and West's eyes turned to water. Radford was going to give them both barrels.

'They didn't expect it,' he said, now standing, the battle re-enacting. 'The Republicans. They had not counted on our Abraham prancing over the hill, arms full of guns, wearing no trousers. Caught them off guard, it did. Must have been an exalted sight, Abraham, all red-faced and bare-bottomed. He'd taken out fifty men, three horses and one unfortunate aardvark before the enemy even considered a counter-attack. They reacted too slowly, too conventionally.

'By the time options were weighed and orders given, our twin-tin-hatted champion had already legged it back over the ridge. One retaliatory shot, that's all they got in. Our beloved Abe, his right bum grazed as he tripped over a well-concealed boulder. The author of his demise was dull old sepsis.' Having dived over the stump of a headstone, Radford slowed his performance and walked carefully back to sit beside West. 'Abraham Butcher,' Radford finished. 'Drunk, hero, Englishman.'

'Drunk, hero, Englishman!' the others recited. They cheered and all was deemed too fantastic.

Brass stuck his drink under his arm and gave rowdy, endorsing claps. 'I thought you was the shy one.'

Over the forthcoming half-hour, to begin the proof of his point, Radford plunged a hand into his outer coat's pocket, took smoke after smoke and the endlessly proffered drinks, and proceeded to say not a single word. The others made noise in his place and became an increasingly dizzy loop. It was all haze and ash and dipping foreheads, time surrendered without notice. The group grew quiet and content: even Rich was lost in contemplation. Radford and West exchanged glances, easy and unafraid.

A bird shivered to rest on the arm of a leaning cross and in that act the world became one of consequence again. It became cold like Radford had never known. Rich made renewed threat of returning to the house and the others finally deemed him sensible.

They were hard-going, those first steps. The boys were drunk. Abraham Butcher drunk. West had his arm around Radford's head.

'It's all jokes, see. You're part of it. Friends play, so we play.'

Invisibly, Radford battled and rejoiced. To hide or confess. He gave a parting salute and hurried on as nimbly as his tragic legs could manage.

Travelling as one, they stumbled, raised their fists and chanted.

'Drunk, hero, Englishman!'

The afternoon was spent secreting their condition from the household. When challenged they would blame their brilliant cheeks and uneasy gait on having been caught by the blizzard while attending to repairs of the chicken house. Lillian had scolded them as they tumbled gaily on the floor of her kitchen.

'The state, let me smell you. Pigs, you've fallen in the vinegar barrel. Get away, shower and change. You offend me.'

She had attacked Brass with a wire brush and the group dispersed. Hours later they had turned expressionless. Most hid in their rooms while Rich, unable to contend with the coop, was asleep on the floor at Radford's bed. It was not the first time: come night Rich was passed around and protected, sleeping at the feet of beds, though in the day he had adopted a stubborn pride in occupying his quarters. Radford sat against the wall, unable to lose consciousness. His ears were hot and his muscles failed to rest. What to do with a changing mind – of intending one thing at departure and finding the vessel altered at arrival?

The tide of night rose over the house and the sorry ones coalesced in the dining room. Radford took an aspirin offered by Brass from across the table. Foster came by as if to say something, but as he did he hit the edge of their table with his hip, spilling water from their glasses.

'Damn it.' Brass flamed with an anger that was too strong.

Foster first apologised but then grew in courage. 'Forget you.'

'Likewise, easily done. Honestly, why can't you vanish? I mean disappear forever.' He brought a fist to his mouth, allowed it to blossom and blew.

'Is that what you'd like?'

'It is. Truly, I would be in heaven.'

West made to start at some nursing peace but Brass shouted it down. The others turned weakly away, like this was a tired scene. Foster looked to be making some calculation of how much this would be worth as Brass rose, making an artificial climax of it.

'The end of you, Foster, would be ecstasy.'

Knowing he had lost, Foster deliberated only briefly before taking Brass's drinking glass and smashing it against the wall. No-one but Radford flinched at the firework of water and amber shot. The explosion took with it the room's tension as Foster retreated and Brass raised his fingers in a V, returning to his beginnings of a cigarette.

Radford could make no decision on Brass. The boy was difficult and enviable but when it came to this elusive Foster he was cruel. There seemed to be nothing Foster could do: it had to be something already past, something corrosive between them.

The room filled as the lusty fire lured more boys to it. Radford was with each spent day becoming more aware of the other house groupings. A boy he recognised from Manny's lesson and five others with long, untidy hair were one. They stood in corners and talked of music, always a record in hand. They would turn it over, pointing to names on the sleeve, making claims, disputing in falsettos.

Another clan, larger and more consuming, was staffed with boys of a striving, physical bent. They jogged, never walked. One would have a ball and the others seemed occupied only with the desire to become that boy. They would stage destructive matches in the upstairs hallway. The previous day, one of them had taken an elbow to the face and this had left a gush of blood the length of the first floor to the toilet. He was now sat close to the fire and holding court, a rim of dark purple still visible around his nostrils. This group hung from each other, their names attached to other names. Leeroy and his Devils. The Slattery brothers, walking forever down a hallway, talking forever about the Blues. Radford had to his credit only those short weeks when he had attached posters of footballers to the wall space above his bed. They had been tolerated, encouraged, until that day they were torn down amid all the screaming.

A boy called Rabbit was standing on the centre of a table, weaving and ducking, shadow boxing and building to the delivery of the great knock-out that licensed his gang to erupt.

He had won, Rabbit.

Rich arrived, holding his back and temple. 'I can't continue. I cannot sleep on another floor or freeze out there with the bloody chickens. I'm finished.'

He went beside Brass, who obliged with the miming of a pistol under his chin. The trigger was pulled and Rich flopped dead onto the table as Teddy stamped in.

'Pigs, boys, now.' He clapped his hands. 'Give me quiet this one time.' Registering the uncommon seriousness of Teddy's tone the room turned still. 'I am tired. Tired of boys coming to me with complaints of debt. We have spoken on this matter, you all know me on this. This house does not respect a loan. You do not lend, you do not offer security. You have obligations – great, whopping ones – but these are never financial. The making of debt mocks your duty to each other.'

The fire roared on, hissing as its flames discovered moisture. Eyes drew down and Brass gave Teddy a discomfited blink of concession.

'As of now,' Teddy said, 'any debt you boys are currently holding between each other is doubled. Hear me? Doubled. And reversed.'

Cries and protestations.

Teddy only reaffirmed his command, waving down the noise. 'Any not abiding can pack a case. Let this be the bloody end.' He left for the stairs.

Brass ran his fingers through Rich's hair. 'That splendid whisky, how much did I owe you?'

Rich pushed one fist into the table, the other into his mouth.

It was three in the morning: three hours, Radford reminded himself, into the reincarnated New Year. Midnight had come with subdued but contented revelry, Teddy having lightened. He allowed a nip for each resident from two dusty bottles of King's Ginger that he had presented ten minutes out from twelve. It was strange, spicy stuff but the boys took it graciously, all relieved that his earlier huff had cooled.

Outside, the wind was wrathful and keeping the house in a constant shake. Tiles and shutters kept up an unremitting chorus as frigid air rushed through the rooms, having found some new and stealthy way inside. Despite this, Teddy had been convinced by Lillian that postponing the New Year for a second time would set an unhelpful precedent. He grew steadily merrier as the night proceeded until in a flash of shushing and excitement he called for all to gather around. He went to the side of the fireplace, where on a small table was a reel-to-reel machine and his radio.

'Manny very kindly made a recording of last night's broadcast. Seems the rest of the world carried on.'

Careful adjustments were confirmed. Manny pushed a button and the room was called to attention by a loud clunk, then a beginning of static.

'Ladies and gentlemen, in a few moments you can hear Big Ben ringing out the old year and ringing in the new.'

There was the tune of Ben's chimes and its dozen bongs, separated by a reverential pause. Teddy struck a fist into the air with each, as though this were all a plan of his devising and going fabulously. After the twelfth note the recorded choir started desperately into 'Auld Lang Syne'. Teddy tried to enlist an ensemble but the boys booed the proposition and returned to their conversations and the last residue of King's Ginger. The adults joined Teddy's song. Lillian, Manny and those staying to give lessons: the historian and the accountant. Farmer Gall was tending the fire, the man now properly steeped and turned sweet.

By three o'clock the jollification had burnt itself out. All the boys but Radford and Rich had retreated to their rooms. Of the elder class just Manny and Teddy remained and, clearly, Manny had been building the courage to retire for at least the previous hour. Teddy had him explaining magnetic tape and the workings of his machine.

'You're putting on a lesson tomorrow?' Radford asked, letting the bait drift out to Manny.

'Oh … yes. I was thinking of it.'

'Looking forward to it. In the morning. Early.'

Manny looked apologetically to Teddy.

'Of course,' came the reply. Teddy slapped his shoulders. 'Get away, promptly. Early start.'

Manny gave Radford an expression like appreciation and bustled to the stairs. Teddy was rubbing his hands, adjusting his coat sleeves, busying every limb.

'Still awake?' he asked.

'No, Teddy,' Rich said without lifting his head from the tabletop. 'I'm toasty in a room of my own. Grander than anything you've imagined. Gold trim, satin, the works. And I do not, in any sense, share it with a score of stinking chickens.'

'What is he talking about?'

'The coop, Teddy.'

'You're not keeping yourself out there?'

Rich lifted his chin.

'You're making a joke.'

'No, Teddy. Not a joke, not at all.'

'It would be absolutely impossible. Suicidal. What possessed you?'

'I can come in?' Rich was straining forward, hovering above the chair.

'Of course, don't be so daft. I know for a fact there's a second mattress in Rabbit's room. Bunk in there for a start.'

Rich leapt to the man, planting an outlandish kiss on the point of his head.

'Get away.' Teddy swished at Rich, who had already spun and fled. 'Very silly.'

So the last pair. Radford had his chin propped in his hands while Teddy shifted from elbow to elbow. In a plea for attention the fire let out a feeble pop.

'Shall I put another log on?'

'Maybe,' Radford said. 'I should go to bed. I feel awful.'

'How so?'

'Nothing really. Tired.'

'Oh, right.'

They stared at the same knot of wood in the table's surface.

'A bit that way myself,' Teddy said. His eyelids seemed made of paper, like they might peel away.

'Which way's that?'

'Awful.'

Radford had first imagined the Manor to be a poisonous place, tough and maybe impossible. Now he didn't know the shape of things. Any time the edges seemed to be becoming clear they would retreat into steam, with this man the least distinct edge of all.

'What's the matter?' Radford asked.

'I suppose I'm tired too.'

More nodding.

'The Royal Oak,' Radford said. 'I was wondering if that was supposed to be a lesson.'

'How would it be?'

'Is it something you do with all the new boys – take them to the end of the grounds and tell them a story about a tree?'

Teddy's eyes narrowed.

'That's fine,' Radford went on. 'If that's what you do. If there's a message, about an ordinary tree that could be great.

I supposed I was meant to find a lesson in it. To consider my place in history or what can come from small beginnings.'

'An inspiring tale?'

'Something like that.'

'You have me wrong.' Teddy smiled and it brought hidden years to his face. 'I have dominion over a very few tasks here. They are to pay the bills and speak with whoever it is from the government that I am required to on any given day. I am to create and file a great quantity of paperwork – that is my most pressing purpose.'

Radford accepted this and turned to the dying fire.

'Do not take that as a measure of my concern. For you all. I am interested in nothing but the fate of you gruesome animals. But I am not the one who will give you what you need.'

'Yes, I've heard this. I'm answerable to myself. I'm the only one who can take responsibility, I know.'

'My god, no.' Teddy took Radford's hands in his. 'Who told you that? What a pile of arse. How are you supposed to look after yourself? You're a sad little ant. A child. Do you not see? You're to look after each other.'

Water was pooling in the corners of Teddy's eyes and Radford could not measure if it was only from the smoke and late hour. The fire let forth with another pop, this time much louder, impersonating its younger self, and he was released from Teddy's hold.

'Off to bed,' Teddy said. 'You have a lesson first thing, if you haven't forgotten. Our dreams run ahead of us, do your best to catch them up. I'll put on a last log.'

So Radford did run, to bed and to sleep, and that night was met by a nightmare that had not found him in years. The one that posed as flying but ended in falling, and left his bed damp and his hollow sarcasm reduced to a filthy sweat across his skin. This dream, the last time, had been a warning.

THREE

It earnt a name: The Big Freeze. What had for a time been a decent cold snap, a playful white Childermass for the romantic, had grown to be a national wreck. The news of it made its way to the Manor by radio and newspaper, though the state of things could be guessed through any window.

Travel to the village became near impossible with the boys' few bicycles rendered useless. The hike was such an unattractive prospect that whisky and tobacco supplies dried to nothing. The house was tense with sober need. Farmer Gall would give lend of his cart and two horses or his rusted Humber Snipe when it would agree to turn over. This saved the house from true isolation as the snow worsened daily.

They would wait for breaks in the wind, every second or third day as need for food arose, with Teddy and Manny up front and two short-strawed boys backwards in the wagon or sat in the car's rear clinging to shovels. When these foraging parties returned it was to relief and hot drinks and much hurrying to the fireside. They would bring bread and milk and whatever quantity of meat the butcher would ration. There were times they returned abundant, others where they scurried inside with a single miserable loaf and a stack of outdated newspapers.

West became town crier. He would teeter on an apple box atop the long table nearest the dining-room fire and read aloud the headlines and columns. Weeks went on and even the harder, affectionless boys would gather.

WORST FOR 82 YEARS – MORE TO COME!

He told stories of trains freezing solid and refusing to regain motion. Vegetables and fuel ran low all over and hamlets were being cut off. Rock salt for the roads ran out after the first week. An old woman gone to walk her dog was found dead. Five others, younger, discovered lost after a whiteout. Two more were suffocated taking shelter in a van. Rubbish mounted in the streets as garbage men were rebranded as snow-clearing teams and sent to make a way through prioritised towns and junctions.

BIGGEST BLACKOUT YET HITS BRITAIN

Power was being cut and afternoons lit by oil lamp. Some were building fires inside, without fireplaces, without chimneys. Houses were burning and people were discovered choked to silence by their desperation.

IT'S CHAOS!

The sea had frozen off Essex. This was the news that hit Teddy hardest. After four weeks of West reporting the abandoned families, the army rescues, the starving horses, the ice turning villagers into inhabitants of fearful islands, it was this news of the ocean turning solid that forced muteness on the man. Until then Teddy had been the house commodore, marshalling and resourceful, but as feet walked out onto the sea his face drained of adventure.

They didn't see him for three days after that.

Manny and one of the stranded teachers took charge as well as they could, directing what limited actions were available and settling disputes. The boys assumed Teddy to have gone to the city but there was talk that he had been seen drifting between the kitchen and his rooms in the very early hours. He returned one day at breakfast, giving no excuse or comment, and by the end of that morning's oats things had resumed an anxious normality. Teddy announced that a little glum weather was no excuse for a fruitless day and that lessons were to continue unfettered. After wash-up he would be giving a tutorial on the subject of leg-before-wicket.

'These bats and ball separate us from barbarism,' he said, rising. 'Lewis, fetch what we need and meet in the hall.'

Even Teddy's eyes were unconvinced by his warming tone. Radford saw this but followed like the others. More of this toxic *sport*. Even those who didn't play, or shouldn't, seemed compelled to develop philosophical interests in the thing. Perhaps it was a way of coping: team as family, opposition as enemy.

Cricket was war and so he would be Switzerland.

*

West made all the actions of opening the door yet it would not shift. 'Give us a hand.'

Radford stepped up and they synchronised their attack.

And a-one – two. The door broke away at one of its hinges and bared the source of resistance. Snow was piled against the outside, scraps of it crumbling into the hall as they squeezed through the gap. The belfry had been unvisited for weeks, since the Freeze had set in and the store of cigarette material had dutifully turned to atmosphere.

This fading afternoon West had stuck his head into Radford's room and mimed the lighting of a pipe. He held a spade and used this to direct Radford to gather blankets. Outside, West pushed the door back into a closed position as well as it could manage, booting ice against its base. They looked to the sky through the missing ceiling: it was not quite frightening, though cruelly cold and dim. They battled to stay upright, but knowing what it could be they fell into a pact of silent gratitude, content to be venturing out at all. Radford wrapped West in a blanket and took one for himself, scraping with his heel to find floor. 'Where'd you get tobacco?'

'Volunteered for the village. Nearly ended belly-up, truly. Got stuck in a dip and it took an hour to dig the cart back onto the road. I slipped away while Teddy was pleading our case to the greengrocer. Had to get pre-rolled, hope that's acceptable, m'lud?'

Radford showed both palms for the packet and the matchbook.

'The occasion calls for some level of dignity.' West raised the shovel. 'A couple of kingly blood like us. We're short a couple of thrones.'

He laid wildly into the banks of snow. Radford stood back as West cleared the centre, heaping ice rubble against the walls until it spilt from each of the four arch window spaces. West turned the tool and began to beat into opposing stacks. The snow compacted into hard seats with high backs, the corners square against the cutting edge. In a final flourish West folded his blanket into a neat cushion, finishing the grand chair. Radford copied and they found their places facing one another, a princes' caucus.

'As it should be.'

They smoked their cigarettes. Radford slid one out, an exquisite, faultless thing with the strong smell of vanilla and peat. *Senior Service*, the packet read, its logo a navy ship under sail, laurelled and capped with the crown and a pair of gliding seagulls. For the life of those first cigarettes he and West relaxed into quiet meditation, and smoke replaced the dust and lifeless air of the house corridors. It was a rough kind of glory and for a time the cold ceased to be.

'Radford, I need you to enlighten me. If we came from apes, when was it that we evolved shame? I mean, when did we stop licking ourselves clean and begin to shower apart, do you know?'

He attempted no answer and left West to continue pondering. The Freeze and its headlines could not be heard. Winter, he was sure, loved them. It cradled and adored them and they lit fresh with the embers of the last.

'You're looking thin,' Radford said, surprising them both. 'You've lost weight, since I got here.'

Upon saying the words he knew it was true – West had lost pounds, and he'd been lean to begin with – but until then this had been mouthless speculation on Radford's part.

West laughed. He took hold of his smoke, bowing in thought, peering with deep curiosity.

'I can't picture what got you here,' West said.

'No?'

'As far as I can tell it takes two things to end up at the Manor: a reason and a final straw. A feller's reason, well, that can be anything. That's the thing way down in a person that means you can't get along with the regulars. How they diagnose you. You're fundamentally disturbed. You're of a violent disposition. Can't bear to be away from Mummy or you're interested in other boys.'

'Truly?' Radford rubbed his neck. 'So what's my reason?'

'No idea, none whatsoever. Reasons can be buried deep, that's what I'm told. You can't tell by just looking at a person. Also, I don't care a bean. I don't want to know your business, you keep that all wrapped up and warm, but I figure there's got to be a second thing. The final straw. Some *thing* that happens that means your dumb life can't keep going the way it was. Some big old rock that you chuck off the cliff that means the people around you can't be around you anymore. With drips like Lewis and Brass it's not hard to imagine. Lewis is top shelf, and there's little I wouldn't do for him, but he's also a great old moose and it's easy to see him sending his mother through a plate-glass window.'

As West spoke the air around his face grew thick and pale with his warmth. He had his chin in his palm and looked, Radford thought, very much the child king delivered by fate and battles lost.

'But you,' West went on. 'I can't see your final straw.' He

raised his hands in peace. 'And I don't want to know – as I said, that's your business. But I must say, I'm intrigued. I am entirely intrigued.'

Radford stretched and a sense of ease shot through him, like Rich's whisky. It felt like a natural and good thing to be under the consideration of another and he thought of telling all to West, if only because he didn't want to let go of this pleasure. Of being in any way fascinating. A series of corrupt, bulky words assembled themselves at the base of his tongue but West drew on his cigarette, released the weakest of coughs, and this was enough to disturb the spell.

'And what about you?' Radford asked.

'Yes, sir?'

'Your final straw. You say you can't imagine mine.'

As he watched West smile and flex his thin arms in the style of a circus strongman, he considered again the weight this boy had so clearly parted with. Pickings from the village were slim but his loss had a more sickly character.

'I might surprise you,' West said.

'You burnt down your school.'

West's laughter was so urgent it sent his cigarette spiralling into the snow. 'Why would you think that?'

'I can picture it,' Radford said.

'Me, burning down a school?'

'Or a church. Did you burn down your church? I can see it. I will confess, I'm intrigued. I am entirely intrigued.'

West clapped and drew two fresh Senior Service, offering one. They returned to their smouldering reverie as the cloud above made its presence known. In the preceding minutes the sky had nudged closer to night and storm. The boys had their heads tilted back and Radford imagined they were breathing in the scent of change, blowing out a fog of human exhaust in retaliation. These two elements would meet in the air above and new would fight old, like it made any difference. Like it would not all become old regardless.

Radford thought of his last straw and dreamt of West's. If it all became the past in the end then what did it matter? All the same, West had been intrigued. Radford tried to remember the sweetness. He closed his eyes and faced the darkening sky, spiting it.

*

'He's back. Snuff, he's back!'

It was Rich ricocheting down the hall. No other's voice could have been so crudely joyous at that hour of the morning. The clock at Radford's bedside showed both hands pointing near six: he hoped that Rich had justifiable cause. The voice trailed away and was replaced by cursing and footsteps. Radford dressed quickly and joined them, seeing Brass and West.

'What was he saying?'

'Snuffy.'

'What's Snuffy?'

The crowd swelled against their backs and pushed to the stairs. They reached the ground floor sounding as flamingos and Rich could be only faintly heard as the colony assembled by the dining-hall fire. Boys competed to attend to the fledgling flames. They prodded and fanned. They bickered over which was the most suitable of the split logs drying against the hearth.

Still no explanation. Still all this inside knowledge.

West pushed through and launched himself at someone sitting in the fireside armchair. Radford moved in and saw an embarrassed West gathering himself from the floor, the chair occupied by a bedraggled pair, a young woman in a young man's lap. She was shivering with purple lips. Beneath her the other figure was equally pale and somewhat more soaked.

Brass made way. 'Snuff,' he declared, initiating a handshake that became a rough hug. 'What state are you in?' He pushed his hands through the other's sopping hair and seemed to first notice his partner.

She gave him a vinegared look and said, 'Victoria,' at the encircling faces, of which a few confessed recognition.

There was much shuffling and half-nodded greeting. West had recovered and he now took Victoria's hand, shaking it firmly enough that water sprang from her sleeves. As he was wiping droplets from his brow and forgetting to release her hand, Rich arrived laden with towels.

'Thank you,' she said and wrapped her hair, then Snuffy's, while hugging another.

West took a self-conscious position at the side of the fire, struggling to settle there. 'We could have sent the cart into the village,' he said. 'If we'd known.'

'The fault's mine,' Snuffy said. 'We found a lift out of London but the off-roads were cut and we ended up pleading our case to a copper with a road crew. Told him we had a place figured out above a pub in the village. He pushed us out at The Black Bear and it was after midnight. Legged it from there.'

He became bashful as Victoria brushed water from his neck. He was the eldest in the room, early twenties, with some of the greater presence and all the weariness that bestowed. She looked a similar age, but those few years seemed to have given Victoria what they had taken from Snuffy.

A woman and a man, Radford knew, but he could not escape the thought of them as girl and boy.

'You could have died,' he said.

He had meant this to sound jovial, congratulatory even, but it induced only quiet and the reactions of Rich and Brass suggested he had trodden an unwelcome path. Even West looked betrayed.

'Got me bang to rights there. It was rightly daft,' Snuffy said. 'What's your name?'

'That's Radford,' Rich said. 'He's new.' *New* said with a weight of apology the word had never before been asked to carry.

'I'm a Manor boy,' Snuffy explained. 'Well, was. Teddy had me stay on, employed me, like. Bit of a tinkerer, do odd jobs and the sort.' Victoria sneezed into a towel and Snuffy went coy. 'Thought I could get us from the village a mite quicker, even in the dark. I've done that trek home from The Black Bear enough.'

Rich took a step forward. 'Remember when we pinched that barrel and rolled it back and the fields were all mud?'

'I remember.'

'You had that Chrissie in tow and she wouldn't stop wailing until you put her up on your shoulders.'

There was a circle of laughter but it stopped short as the boys caught Snuffy's objecting stare, his eyes flitting to Victoria.

'So noble,' she said. Healthy colour had returned to her lips.

'Thought you had a stretch left,' Brass said.

'Teddy. They told me Teddy fixed it.'

'So, how was it?' Rich attempted a serious tone.

Snuffy went to speak but pulled the words back. There was some sombre agreement and West's mouth closed in assent. Radford thought better of asking his question.

'Bird,' Snuffy said calmly to Radford. 'Just did six months.'

Victoria faced Radford. 'He's incredibly hard now he's been to gaol. Hard and impressive, you didn't know?'

Brass piped in. 'Thought you got a year and a half?'

'Teddy, once again.' He reached to retrieve Victoria's palm.

Radford felt the urge to repay her for something he couldn't identify. He considered if this was his fate, to be enraptured and turned stupid by the mere presence of those with personality.

'Simon?' This was Teddy at their side, re-tying his dressing-gown belt and patting its pocket.

Snuffy motioned to stand.

'Stay, you're drenched. You haven't dared walk here?'

The pair bowed their heads and Teddy huffed and signalled for the boys to push the armchair closer in on the flames.

'Victoria, isn't it?'

'It is. Thank you and I'm very sorry to have arrived like this and caused such a fuss.'

'I'll ask Lil to find you some dry things. And can someone please fetch some tea?'

Snuffy was red with sin.

'They told me they would let me know when to expect you.' Teddy was pacing. 'I was going to arrange a car. You could have killed yourselves. I'll be calling my man at the prison, I promise. I'm terribly cross at you, Simon.' His pipe found home and he struck a match. 'Terribly.'

Smoke encircled them, overtaking the humid puffs of the hearth, and Teddy called for the gathering to break. Radford watched the final adoring gazes, all fixed on this veiled, unslept Snuffy, all somehow denying Victoria.

'To work?' Teddy said, snapping the room from its fantasy. 'Simon?' This made the man definitively a boy and a wide smile surfaced. 'When you're dressed, I believe Lil is being given trouble by her ovens.'

She arrived with the sound of her name, pushing past Radford, throwing arms around Snuffy.

'Morning, Lilly.'

She retracted. 'Who are you to call me that? After you leave us for so long. All these days.'

'Of course. Miss Grange.'

She helped the hair back from Victoria's face. 'Darling, you are so cold. Your skin is frozen to the touch.' She glared at the boys. 'You silly pigs have brought no tea?'

Lillian snatched a towel and draped it around Victoria's knees before kissing her forehead. She gripped Snuffy by the ear and drew their brows together.

'My Snuffy, you have never been in this kind of trouble. I have never been angrier,' Lillian said. 'Never been so furious.'

She kissed his hand ruthlessly.

FOUR

Radford had overslept. Upon hearing the distant tinkle of breakfast bowls being stacked he felt that monstrous sensation of having missed out. Despite any obvious need to do so, the house woke incessantly early. The boys were up just after the sun, with Lillian already in the kitchen, porridge warm and bread toasted, always before the first of them drifted down. As Radford pulled on his clothes it occurred to him that she might be driving this dawn-abiding enterprise. She might believe that early rising was in some way Provençal.

He would ask West.

This late morning few souls remained in the dining room and they were sat by the radio, fed. He rushed to the kitchen to see Lewis and another working the dishes, both in elbow-length rubber gloves and sweating over copper boiling pots.

'You have errored,' Lillian said and moved ahead to scratch her nails through Radford's temples. 'You are very lazy and very late and that is why you should starve.'

'Yes.'

She gripped him by the nape of his neck. 'I am a soft-hearted fool and I am weak. I have saved you a bowl and two slices.'

Radford went for the oven and then scooted from the room. He went to the edge of a dining table by the warmth and started into his limp toast, the radio boys glancing at him before returning to their news. The presenters spoke as all of their kind did; that they were wearing suits was obvious from their intonation. His mother had taught him that, about the newsreaders bothering to dress. She had told him as an amusement but also, he supposed, as demonstration of the taking of pride. It was a game he suspected he was skilled at, inventing lessons from his mother. He moved on to the porridge with its hardened skin as the newsmen spoke of the Freeze.

The fiercest falls yet had swept over the island and raged for a day and a half without respite. Great drifts had deposited atop cities. Wind had removed roofs and taken down walls. With the worsening weather Radford had noticed frustration showing itself more regularly in the Manor, fights and shouting matches bursting like sparks but extinguishing as quickly. An effort was being made, coiled punches held back.

Radford finished his meal and delivered the dishes into Lewis's side of the sinks. The radio's call grew faraway and hollow as he conquered the house. He wondered about West and the others. There had been talk of Teddy mounting an expedition to the village and that new straws would be drawn. The tobacco situation was beyond critical: even West's secret stash was almost to nothing. The pair had taken to their smoking thrones only twice over the last few days, it having been too difficult to peel away undetected. Lewis had caught them the day before as they were nearing the belfry door and they had been forced to ad-lib a routine about getting some air. When Lewis insisted on joining, the three of them pushed their way outside and stood pointlessly raw. West had taken huge breaths, puffing his chest out in search of credibility.

Radford reached the empty Long East Room. He would throw his hand up for the expedition. He owed something to each in the group, none more than West, and coming through with the smokes would go a long way towards absolution. It was only as he turned to leave, just as he was becoming sure of the cheers and slaps that would accompany his successful village return, that he noticed Manny rise from behind the table.

'Oh, good morning.'

The man corrected his spine as if responding to a warden's call.

'Just saying *good morning*,' Radford explained.

Mollified, Manny returned to his leather case, full with tubes and valves, all strapped and tied in place.

'Are you giving a lesson?'

'Was to,' Manny said, his eyes staying down. 'Teddy asked me. No-one came.'

Again Radford envisaged his triumph. Of the house door being blown open by hurtful wind to reveal the expeditioners bound down by their meat and milk and loaves. All the household would praise their obvious bravery, and at the peak of excitement he would loosen the strap to his shoulder bag and show West and the others its contents: a pouch, several pouches – perhaps a small canvas sack – of tobacco. This was not the repayment of debt, this was the making of a fresh god.

He thought of glory and kindness, what it took to crown or destroy a person.

'Sorry I'm late,' Radford said. 'Only just got breakfast.'

Manny ceased the packing of the remaining device, a black box with leather handles and a banana-shaped face. 'Late?'

'Very late, I'm sorry.' Radford looked as directly as he could muster into the man's doggy eyes.

Manny flinched, smiled, flinched again. He turned his attention to the box. 'Know what this is?'

'No.'

'What does it look like?'

'Thermometer?'

'Why would it be a thermometer?'

'No idea, Manny.'

'What does it say?'

He lowered to the device. 'It says *amp* … ah, *amp-eres* and *The Walsall Electrical Company*.'

'And what's measured in amperes, or amps?'

'I don't think I know.' After a few seconds Radford straightened and added a shake of his head. 'No, sorry. No idea at all. Something … well, *electrical*?'

'You came for the lesson?'

'That's right.'

A just-perceptible twitch came to the man's eye. 'Perhaps I could show you a few of the basics.'

And so for the rest of the morning Manny instructed on the fundamentals of electronics. Footsteps galloped about them, from the floor above and the adjacent hallway, which after a time Radford ceased to acknowledge. There were only Manny's words with their subtle lisp. Just wires and what they could bring together.

Relays, switches, transformers.

He admired their size and density, their miniature perfection. Manny took a vacuum tube from its sleeve and placed it in Radford's hands, telling him to hold it high to the daylight. It was the shape of an odd lightbulb stretched thin and long, with the glass darkened at its end. Inside was a tiny galaxy of silver and copper with small rectangles of black. It was arranged in exacting symmetry, everything being made parallel or sent off at a neat right angle, and Radford savoured its surprising weight. Manny described its function with words like *anode* and *cathode*, and became animated as he defined the process of *black body radiation*.

On many occasions Radford's uncle had attempted to interest him in car mechanics. He had spent weekends being shown the passage of oil and petrol and exhaust. He had passed wirecutters and cloths and socket wrenches on command. Three times he had watched a carburettor disassembled, carefully laid out on a drop sheet, cleaned, dried, then reassembled. Three times he had failed to be moved by the experience. Here with Manny, however, he wanted to know all these mysterious articles and to befriend them.

'Resistor,' Manny said and placed it on the table.

This was the most pleasing curiosity yet, consisting of just a small tube with a stiff wire protruding from each end. All told it was the length of a matchbook and the tube bore four coloured bands, each to be deciphered: brown, green, orange, silver.

There was a chart: first number, second number, multiplier, tolerance.

One, five, three, ten.

After discussion and correction Radford announced it to be a fifteen-thousand-ohm resistor with a tolerance of ten per cent.

'A fifteen-K,' Manny agreed.

Radford did not know what ohms were or if fifteen thousand of them was at all a reasonable amount. He did not know what this resistor was ten per cent tolerant of but knew that he was quite properly in love.

'Christ, I've spent all morning looking—' West stood at the doorway, having halted himself. 'Oh. Sorry, Manny.'

'Fifteen-K,' Radford explained and turned on his stool.

West smiled queerly, coming closer. 'Of course,' he said. 'Manny, I'm looking to steal him away. Have you finished?'

Radford eyed the resistor.

'We've finished,' Manny said.

West pulled Radford to his feet and they walked from the room. Tiny fires of his heart fought to stay lit.

'Thank you,' he said over his shoulder, to which Manny gave a twitch and a nod.

It was all secretive fuss as they squeezed through a football game in a cramped downstairs room, moving to the kitchen. West remarked to Lillian that they were going out to chop wood.

'Oui,' she said, draping a tea towel over her face. 'Should

not take you long with all the help. Chopping wood is what all the others said.'

The stinging outer world met them as a gust slammed the door shut. West directed them close to the exterior wall. 'Don't worry, she wouldn't grass.'

At the building's end they stopped at a door that, in Radford's time, had always been behind a robust chain and lock.

'Off limits, strictly speaking,' West said. 'But what does Teddy expect? How are we to nurture our rebellion?'

He triumphed over the handle and the door fell open to shouting from inside about the cold. He bowed, rolling his hand for Radford to lead on.

'Took your time,' Brass said.

West shook away his snow. 'He was building a robot with Manny.'

Rich put a cigarette into Radford's mouth, encouraging him onto a floor cushion against a wall as West took the place opposite.

'Worthy warrior, welcome to our tents,' Snuffy said from the far end obscured by haze.

A velvet sheet was nailed to the ceiling in some attempt to conceal a bed. Opposite that was a toilet that made no effort to hide, alongside a sink and tin bath. The space that remained was taken with scarred furniture, clothes, and collections of rubbish that seemed to have been recently swept into mounds. Snuffy was sprawling around a record player. Albums lay in arcs and he and Lewis were examining one of their sleeves, the thing flexing under their scrutiny. In the air was wild sound: Radford hadn't heard music like it though he recognised drums and a lone horn. All was afire and everyone drank the same dark something. Brass handed him a glass and a second lit stick.

'Rich went with the boss to town. And he came through, got to hand it to him.'

Radford showed Rich a salute and the other boy blew a roof-bound plume, exceptionally pleased. West asked Radford his opinion of the tune and of Snuffy's apartment.

'Wonderful,' Radford said and saw Snuffy gaze up from the vinyl. 'Nice digs.' He cringed as these awful words escaped him.

'Thank you, my man. Consider them yours.'

Radford took a slug of the liquor as a cast-iron heater let out a hiss and he saw that not all of its smoke was finding exit through the stovepipe. A significant fraction was leaking through a crack where the pipe turned into the wall and this was joining the tobacco's cloud, leaving all the room a slate mist. The record player jumped then rediscovered its uncivil rhythm.

It was all so soothing Radford thought he might really cry – like a weakling, like a bore – and so buried his head behind his arm and waited for the urge to pass.

Rich jabbed him. 'Has us down whenever we're able, when we won't be pinched right away. Gets records in from the city. Snuffy,' he called, 'who's this?' He swirled his finger into the sound.

'Dizzy.'

'To Dizzy,' West said, motioning for the room to similarly extol.

They repeated the call, falling hopeless in trying to meet glasses and complete the toast just as the door came open and allowed in a surge of sharp cold. Victoria. She shifted the hair from her face. A hand was left on her hip as she examined the mess of humanity spilling across the carpet.

'You've reverted to beastliness,' she said. 'I was only gone a minute.' She went by and took West's glass, finishing his drink. 'Pleased to see it, be beasts.' She ruffled West's hair, refilled his glass and returned it.

Lewis attempted another toast, 'Beasts!', which, quite rightly, inspired no response.

Victoria sat to Snuffy's side and they were soon arguing and blowing smoke away from each other's faces. Glasses knocked and paper continued to roll. Laughter and more saluting of Rich. It went on much like this for the remainder of Dizzy Gillespie and both sides of the Cannonball Adderley Quintet. This last record had brought quiet to Radford: not melancholy or anger, just a desire for silence. When Victoria squeezed down between him and Rich he had been contemplating that he had no idea what whisky was made from, and he would make sure that he never found out.

He shook hands with her. 'Haven't been here long, have you?' she asked. 'I'd only known these others for a little while, a few weeks before Snuffy went away. Last summer.'

'You were allowed to stay?'

'Just for a short time. Teddy found me the first morning and took me for a walk. We understand each other, a little at least.'

'Did he show you the oak?'

'What's that – should he have?'

He settled deeper into his cushion, retracting the urgency of his question.

'He might have,' she said. 'It was a long walk and I was a little confused. He certainly talked of birds.' They laughed as Rich refilled their glasses and Victoria proposed a new tribute. 'To the birds.'

As their drinks met Radford noticed the hair at her temple seemed to be coming away from the scalp.

'Are you okay?' He reached without thinking and she pulled her head back, panicked. 'I'm sorry, I didn't mean to—'

'Don't worry.' She fixed the hair, pressing her thumb at her forehead, calming. 'Thank you.'

All at once she seemed so familiar and he could not understand why. They talked about music and Radford saw no reason to pretend: he told her he knew nothing of it. She applauded this, saying that she knew everything about it but only enjoyed the tunes that Snuffy thought were obvious. She asked if he preferred sport or art or books.

'No, none of those.'

'So what do you think about?'

He pondered this for some time, gazing into the ceiling cloud, and she began to fit with laughter.

'West is your good friend?' She pointed to where he was playing cards with Lewis.

'What do you mean?'

'He's been looking to see if you're okay.'

'Oh, right. I'm still on your last question.'

The ceiling continued to offer no assistance.

'Your eyes,' she said. 'They are so blue.'

'They're brown.'

'I say they're blue.'

They talked of other things, of how well each other did or did not sleep and whether they thought in full sentences or a mush of ideas. Her hair, again, came away from her skin and he let it be. Just so familiar. He wanted to have his eyelids come closed and yet be able to see. He wanted so much to swim backstroke above them through the smoke. To meet her by sightless senses.

The door heaved open. Teddy stood tired and holding himself together against the gale. 'All right, you pigs,' he said quite happily and made beckoning gestures outside.

A thin shirt was visible beneath his dressing-gown, which he clutched to keep together. His slippers were wet and caked. Snuffy stood and with no conviction hid the whisky behind his back.

'Yes, yes,' Teddy said. 'What surprise. Come, one and all, we know the procedure. Must we persist? Let us skip the formalities and return to the house and all get on with our rotten lives. I am too ill, too bored, to go through the tedious dishing out of punishments.'

He remained at the side of the door and presided over the procession of cowards. They all stooped at the point of passing, as if Teddy's sleepy glare threatened to lash them. They all apologised in their way. Some mouthed or squeaked *sorry*. Brass batted himself on the back of the head as he exited. West and Radford gave the least, feeling the worst, shuffling near the doorway while Victoria and Snuffy backed themselves into the fire's corner.

'All me,' Snuffy said, raising his cigarette. 'I'm to blame.'

Teddy's face grew grim, tightening. 'Yes. Yes, you are, Simon. You ruiner.'

'We're so sorry,' West said.

Teddy kept his stare with Snuffy. 'These boys are guests. Simon, you are an employee. Am I correct? I couldn't care less at their behaviour, but you …'

No-one spoke for a time. Music now seemed so juvenile. The red in the old man's face faded and he ran a hand across the back of his neck.

'I'm sorry,' Victoria said. 'Stupid of us. After everything.'

'Oh, good grief,' Teddy said and adjusted his gown cord. 'Let's not get maudlin.' He put his hands on West and Radford, herding them outside. 'But, if the wrong kind of person had visited the house today, well … There are many convinced we're having a great joke out here and would be pleased to see us all out on our arses. Am I right? And none of you thought to invite me.'

'We truly are sorry,' Victoria said, not hearing the joke.

The boys checked each other's faces. Teddy reached out and plucked the smouldering fag from between West's fingers. He took a full, glamorous drag.

'I am only flesh and blood,' he said. 'Only flesh.'

He returned the stub and marched outside, bringing all behind. They were gratefully subjugated, rubbish in the wind.

*

Radford and West had broken away to the belfry, and for three cigarettes they took seat of their thrones. Snuffy had in one way or another been the dominating topic of conversation since the morning of his arrival, but a change had come in the previous twenty-four hours. All had flipped and it seemed the boys were trying to last the longest without breathing his name.

'Snuffy. How old is he?' Radford asked, bowing out of competition.

'Twenty-two.'

They nodded, in quiet reverence to this.

'Are you in love with Victoria yet?'

Radford waved the notion away too vigorously.

'You should be, if you're not,' West said.

'In love?'

'Of course.'

It was a clumsy thought that had occurred to Radford more than once. He wondered if it could be accurate. How pathetic that would be. How *obvious*.

'What would it mean if I was?'

'Nothing at all,' West said.

'I haven't admitted to this.'

'I thought it might be something you'd like to talk about.' West gestured for the matchbook. 'Love is something people want to endlessly discuss, to speak like they might be in a film.' He paused, putting weight on one knee and mimicking a matinee idol. 'I prefer to smoke, it being one of life's elementary pleasures. No courtship. No having to reason with the thing or earn its respect. You introduce it to a flame and …'

He took a drag. 'You breathe. Other pleasures are fine and worth chasing, but to smoke … is to taste life undiluted.'

'How profound. And what of you and love?' Radford asked.

'Of course not.'

'But you say I should.'

'*You* should.'

Evening was hurrying over the house and the sound of bodies piling on the stairs was leaking through the flimsy door. Radford would not give himself up just yet.

'You may have to go on wondering for a while,' he said.

'I will.' Ugly shots of half-melted snow began to fall across West's face. 'Something I haven't told you. My parents are coming.'

'Here? I didn't know – didn't know it was allowed.'

'Of course, just doesn't happen too often. I mean, why would they come?'

'Yours have been before?'

West smiled. 'Three months since my father, six for Mother. And even then she refused to leave the car. *The chill was dangerous.* Jesus – there were butterflies, Radford, butterflies dancing gaily about the sundews. Twenty minutes, they never left the driveway.' He released a cough of laughter. 'Will yours come? Some day?' His smile chewed itself to a grimace.

Radford waited, still and long enough for snow to litter his hair. He had not packed all he needed in his suitcase and would need to ask after a woollen hat. He imagined the snow aging him, making him grey before his time. He wouldn't answer his friend, or even consider the question.

West pushed out of his seat and squinted into the increasing downpour. 'Oh, will you stop?' He shook a fist and gave all his venom to the sky. 'Will you stop the god-sodding snow? Stop the wind. Stop all of this! Winter! You bastard! What is your point?'

He was pushing his knuckles into his sides and looking around his feet for something on which to impose violence. The kick he delivered to his throne was an impressive one and white flew up like dirt after a landed grenade. Radford lunged and gave his own detonative kick. They raised eyebrows in agreement and leapt on the throne, demolishing it with hooves and blows. They were roaring and screeching, lustful in the act of devastation. It was Radford who first picked up a chunk and launched it at the sky. West followed and they were soon frantic, collecting clods of snow and hurling them to the air, over the edge of the belfry walls and out of the light's bounds.

'You will not take us!'

They exhausted all breath and energy and stood facing, leaning into one another.

A fleeting thought came into Radford's mind. Who of the house had been given this attention of West's before his arrival? It seemed real to Radford, but what if it was nothing special and he had simply been the next?

West was able to gather air. 'Did we win?'

'The campaign will be long.'

'Of course.' West was staring into his colourless hands. 'Perhaps we retreat, just for the time being. I can't feel my fingers.'

Together, combining their numb feet and unbending digits, they found a way inside and began a graceless run to the fire.

*

Radford came into the hall. 'They're here?'

That morning West had been a mess, neat but nervous in a way that Radford found infectious. The pair had sent each other into an anxious spiral and in the end West had demanded Radford be sequestered in his room.

'Up in Teddy's now,' Lewis said.

At the staircase the group huddled against the railing, their heads cocked.

'Anything?'

Brass looked up at the disturbance, annoyed.

'Not much,' Rich said in a whisper. 'They went straight in, all serious. Heard a raised voice before, couldn't make it out, the mother.'

The mere squeak of Radford's footstep attracted another glare from Brass.

'The father seems a jellyfish,' Rich said.

There was a mumbling from the floor above and an occasional pair of shifting heels.

The door to Teddy's rooms came open. 'Margot.' This could only have been the father, pleading. 'Margot, stay.'

The boys assembled as she came down clutching her purse, her vision intent on each stair as she negotiated the escape. She passed the gallery without acknowledgement.

'We're not finished, Margot.' The father showed himself. 'There are things to sort.'

He paused at coming level with the group and they feigned indifference. Rich had begun to whistle.

'Boys, good morning.'

'Mr West,' Brass replied and, for reasons unknown to Radford, saluted.

West's father and his placations hurried down after his wife. Teddy came in their wake; West too, without looking up from his sharply polished shoes.

'Come, now,' Teddy said calmly as they descended.

It was unclear if this was a request to follow or a warning to remain but, like the rest, Radford followed. The mother had already made it outside. The boys stood in conspicuous clusters, knowing neither what was happening nor what could be done. Teddy spoke into the father's ear outside the main house door.

'You okay?' Brass asked of West, reaching out, only to have his hand slapped away.

West began to dash frantically about the room as if outrunning a fire. He darted between the boys, pushing each away in turn. He was near crying, his face a ruin, failing to keep breath. Attracted by the ruckus, others were arriving now, and the crowding fanned West's panic.

Foster was one among them and he came ahead and took possession of West by the collar. 'What is it? What's been said?'

At this Brass launched into the pair and swung his fist down, freeing West and sending the hurt Foster back into the surrounding bodies.

Teddy saw the tail end of the conflict. 'Get rid of him.' He pointed to the casualty as he walked back out. 'I don't care where.'

Foster was set upon, his arms trapped. Steered against a wall, the boy delivered a blow to at least one jaw. West looked to his father, who paused briefly before continuing to the car. The mother was already seated on the passenger side. West shoved his way through the room and deeper into the house.

'Leave him,' Teddy said at the doorway as Radford came forward. 'Leave him, please.'

Someone needed to be fixing this, dragging the father back inside while someone saw to West. The mother needed to be extracted from the car, reasoned with. Yet they all just gawped like cows. Radford gave Teddy an accusing leer before running after West. He found him alone in the kitchen, at the sinks, looking out through clouded windows.

'Yes?' West asked.

There was no miracle of thought, nothing to counteract the abandonment. Radford had thought only as far as West being alone and the crime of that.

'I don't know,' he said in the end.

West gave a short-lived smile as Radford went to his side and began to flick absently at the tea towels hanging from the oven handle.

'I shouldn't be shocked that they're leaving,' West said. 'The surprise is that they came at all.' He was rubbing his hand into his chest. 'Did you see her?'

'She looked angry.'

'Teddy told them it was about time I went home.' He laughed. 'Should have seen her. Was like she'd found out she had six weeks to live.'

'You're going home?'

'She said it was a crazy idea. And that I'm still crazy. All the world is mad but Mother.'

The towel and its stains gave no helpful answer. Neither did the leafless trees or Radford's shoe tips. He screwed the towel.

'Come on.' He went straight. 'Let's give a proper goodbye, bon voyage.'

West cringed.

'Make them remember. It's only manners – when people leave, you give a cheerio.'

'Maybe.'

'Like a little kid, waving goodbye on the first day of school. They need to see. It's pointless but it's something for them to remember. After that we go and have a smoke. In our belfry.'

'Okay, yes. Can I just take a minute? I'm going to wash my face. A minute?'

'We'll say goodbye together, all of us. To show them.'

Radford waited at the end of the hall. This would be a sight West's parents could surely not ignore. This would hurt – the son waving farewell, fading into the distance of the rear-view mirror. He wanted their hearts to sting. West reappeared and went by without slowing, making the crowd and then outside. Radford ran after. West got ahead past Teddy and onto the pale stones of the drive while the car was reversing away, the father looking back over his shoulder and the mother's face directed firmly downwards. Radford stood with Lewis and Rich.

'We're going to wave, okay?'

'Why?'

'To irritate that pair of cowards. Right? When West starts we join in.'

They made themselves into a rough line. Teddy took a few leaden steps back to join them and gave what seemed intended as a reassuring shrug.

'Mother!' West was twenty feet ahead and had one hand raised in a slow wave. 'Father!'

'Okay – now.' Radford and the line began to wave ridiculously at the retreating car.

It was just as the vehicle reached the top of the drive and was near to passing through the gap in the stone wall that West removed the knife from his pocket. It was an elegant thing and shone bright and mortal against the clouds. He called merrily and brought the blade down in an unhesitating arc, slashing it against his chest.

Teddy roared. He and Brass were the first to move, breaking the line and dashing forward. Radford stayed at his mark. Others were shouting – names, sounds. West kept one hand up waving, the other with the knife. The red of blood was across its metal, dripping down to the snow and gravel.

West sang for his mother.

Ahead the car halted and the father's door swung open. The mother shouted something unintelligible. Teddy reached the boy first with Brass pulling the weapon from his hand and throwing it into the trees. West was spun around and ended up seated on the ground. His beautiful white shirt, one Radford had never seen him wear, bore a wide crimson slash across its front.

'Get Lil,' Teddy said. 'Someone, get Lil. Tell her to bring her kit.'

Lewis claimed the task and grabbed at Rich's arm. They went against the tide streaming outside. Radford was yet to move as it could achieve nothing. The Manor surged around West and closed a circle. Teddy waved for space and Brass ran ahead, signalling to the parents, screaming at them to stop. The father's door closed and the car reversed to the road: they were gone before Brass made it even half the length of the drive.

Radford said nothing, thought of nothing, just looked down at West. The stripe of red had spread down that beautiful shirt. West looked back and smiled. Such an exquisite shock of colour against the white.

*

He said it had been for attention.

In the days that followed, the house was attended by two doctors, each going first with Teddy to his rooms and then to West, who was being confined to bed. No boys had been permitted to visit and one of the adults was in with him at all times, even at three in the morning when Radford and Brass had attempted and failed at a clandestine raid. The first doctor, the one with the standard grey moustache and leather bag, had been in with West for twenty minutes. The second doctor, with the rounded glasses and notepad, had stayed for most of a day, sitting with West for an hour at a time between taking Teddy for brief meetings.

Conclusions were come to.

It had not been a deep cut and was bandaged and healing. West made promise one final time that it had been only for the attention and this, ultimately, was accepted. He was to stay. The parents had been called and had not returned.

*

Radford hesitated before pushing in the door to Teddy's office. The hunger to speak with him about West had propelled him out of bed and up the stairs but had failed to make clear anything further than the knocking.

'Is it too late?' he asked and waited for the reply.

The clock showed thirty minutes after midnight but Teddy was standing in his suit and the fire was sparking with fresh wood. After completing a lap of the room and giving the globe on the desk an aimless quarter-turn he took to his seat and waved for Radford to occupy the one opposite. He had not set foot in the room since the day of his arrival but, like the others, he had stuck his head around the frame of the open door many times. They stood at the threshold to receive instructions, ask their questions, take receipt of requests and plead their cases. Teddy was granted his rooms. Now Radford sat facing him, not knowing how the conversation might be initiated.

'Oh,' Teddy said as if remembering something. He leant over his desk. 'Here, here – toffee?'

He tilted open a silver box, took one of the small parcels for himself and tossed another into Radford's lap. For a few minutes they sat chewing their sweets to surrender. The shelves of books behind Teddy were all histories. Egyptian, Greek, Roman, British – civilisations laid out, bound in leather and assembled. Wars and their territories all resolved and in order of time's passing.

'You're welcome to these,' Teddy said, noticing Radford's inspection. 'You're interested in history?'

'I'm not sure.' He would have typically answered this kind of question without consideration, either in the affirmative to hurry beyond the scrutiny or in the negative to avoid it, but that night he found truth coming more easily than habit. 'There was the story you told me about the Royal Oak.'

'I have something here.' He began a fingertip along the spines. 'Yes, here we are.' Teddy pulled a book from the line and handed it over. *An Account of the English Civil Wars* by E. N. Seymour. 'Nostalgia disguises itself,' he said. 'Be wary of it.'

Radford spun the book, feeling the grain of the leather and the undulations of sunken letters.

'Each generation feels it stands on the precipice of eternal decline,' Teddy said. 'And every generation has thought that it alone is correct in this judgement. We believe the best is behind us, that there's a time that would suit us better and it's always just gone, just out of reach. Sweet, really.'

'I've come about West.'

'Of course.'

Waiting for one of them to continue Radford became aware

of the clock's dull ticking. The wind joined in, making swoops against the window glass.

'You want to know if he's okay?' Teddy asked.

'I suppose.'

The man produced his pipe and began all its ceremonies. 'It's a fair question and I'm glad you've asked it. I see that you two have become close. The truth about West is that I am not sure.'

Radford waited for this to explain itself.

'Please do not condemn me for this uncertainty,' Teddy said. 'I've been thinking of little else since his performance.'

'Performance? He carved himself open.'

'I know full well.' Teddy showed pain at the accusation. 'When I say *performance* I say it in hope rather than as a dismissal. I want it to have been only a show – for his parents, for us all – because that is something I have seen before and something we can recover from. I cannot tell you that West is okay any more than I can be certain that any of you are. That is not something I can ever be sure of. If I were then I could sleep.'

The recesses of Teddy's face darkened as he allowed the first wraith of smoke to escape his mouth. Radford didn't know how to take his words. He knew only that his worry for West was making him sick in the belly. His chest felt as if it were bound.

'I don't know if I am helping,' Teddy said. 'That is the full truth. But I have to believe the Manor is a better place for West right now than anywhere else. If there were somewhere that I knew could keep West safer he'd be packed and sent in an instant. Please believe me.'

'I do.'

Teddy nodded. 'All we can do is our job. We are all similarly employed, do you see? All on duty and that is all we can be, all we must.'

The last of the smoky toffee lapped Radford's teeth and he thought of what Teddy might mean as the wind lashed again and startled them both. They laughed at each other's fear.

'I'll let you be, Teddy. Thank you for the book.' He patted its cover and stood.

'You keep it as long as you like. Tell me, do you think you'll read it?'

Radford again recognised the easy journey of honesty to his lips. 'I don't know.'

'Just taking it to be polite?'

'That's right.'

Teddy smiled broadly. 'May not be a bad thing if you never read it. The past has powers.' He made wizardly suggestions with his fingers and sucked on his pipe. They both stared into its red centre. 'It is an intoxicant – it is set, you see? No matter how cruel, the past is a fixed and knowable thing and no future can make a claim like that. History, as written, is certain, and that is very attractive. Don't give in.'

Radford made his way out, returning downstairs and hoping for West to be awake. His friend's door was ajar and Radford took this to mean he had yet to attempt sleep but as he pushed it open the vision of West lying unconscious beneath his bedclothes greeted him. It was Radford's involuntary apology that opened West's eyes.

'I'm sorry. The door was … I thought.'

'Don't worry, come in. Come on.'

Radford tried to shut the door but found a square of wood had been fixed to the frame, preventing it from coming fully closed.

'Part of the new deal,' West said, switching on his lamp. 'They had Snuffy nail it in. I can't be trusted with privacy, who knows what I'll get up to?' He mimed slitting his neck.

'Don't joke.'

'Oh Christ, Radford. Really, everyone needs to calm a little. One stupid thing and—'

'You can't be surprised you got a reaction.'

'Of course not, I've admitted that. I'm not the only one who's pulled a stupid trick. Did you know Brass put his head through a plaster wall last year?'

Radford wanted his frustration acknowledged. He could only cross his arms.

'Well, he did, the dolt. Rich saw him. They told Teddy it was from a cricket ball. Wore a cap for a fortnight to hide the crack down the back of his idiotic head.'

'People in glass houses.'

'Clichés now?'

'That's all you're worth.'

'You do know actions speak louder than words?'

Radford stood at the bed's end and grudgingly allowed his grimace to depart. 'But the pen is mightier than the sword.'

'Well, exactly. Confusing, isn't it?'

Radford sat on the mattress corner. 'You can't be mad at people's worry.'

'I'm not,' West said. 'I'm embarrassed.' He adjusted his

pillow and sat higher. 'I feel like a fool, if I'm being honest. What a stupid thing to do. A dumb, dumb thing.'

'Yes.' Radford locked his hands together, warming them. 'But that is it, isn't it? I mean, is this the end of it?'

'Of course.' West's face flushed. 'Of course that's the end.'

'Promise.'

'I promise you.'

Radford refused to crumble. Despite every urging, he would not fold, because it could not help. He thought of Teddy's reminder, of his employment.

'Okay.' He nodded. 'Yes.'

'And you, will you promise?' West took his arm from beneath the covers and extended it, offering a handshake.

'To what?'

'That you're not going to get hurt either,' West said. 'Why don't we … can we say this is the end of stupid business for us both? Let's agree on that. That's not something we do.'

Radford thought of his first night in the house. Of his standing at the edge of the ultimate depth, and West's interruption. 'Okay, yes.'

West gripped tighter, calling for focus. 'No, you have to promise. Indulge me.'

It was a call that made such great demands of Radford's heart, building a pressure in him. The demand to be there. He cursed his soft shell.

'I promise,' Radford said and the pair gave a final, emphatic downstroke as the windows rattled angrily.

Winter held the house by its roof and shook, longing for cracks through which it could plunge its arms and choke these prideful creatures. Its moon face remained without expression. These vainglorious clowns, they would repent.

*

Another doctor arrived, a Dr Cass – and he made clear he was to be thusly addressed. He was brought from the village by Snuffy in a journey that was by both their accounts foul. The roads were under thick snow again, as good as impassable they said, and a man at the butcher's had heard that the clearing gangs weren't expected for at least a week. Cass would be staying. Teddy called all to the dining room and made introductions.

This visitor seemed at once an unforgiving, dubious type. Ashen-skinned, he appeared a similar age to Teddy but his posture spoke of a different provenance. He was evidently angered by the challenges of the journey, and by the sudden proximity of so many boys and their incomplete attention.

Twice during Teddy's announcement Cass called for quiet.

'Ooh-er, will you get *him*,' Brass said too camply and too loud, and Teddy was forced to scold him.

'Sorry, Teddy.' Brass covered his mouth.

Cass flinched at this flagrant use of an adult's name. Teddy explained that the doctor was present to observe and to learn. The doctor's questions were to be answered and he was to be afforded the same respect offered to all of the house staff.

'Bugger-all then,' someone called from the back.

Teddy glared in the direction of the voice and gave Cass an apologetic smile. 'High spirits.'

Cass made for his suitcase and hat and waited to be shown through the sea of insolence. West's group were taken to the kitchen by Snuffy, and Radford learnt that Rich had been asked to bunk in with Lewis to make a spare room. They had screamed murder upon learning of the arrangements.

'He's up to dark things, that Cass,' whispered Snuffy to the completed scrum. 'I tried to juice him for information on the way here. Only got that he wants to *have everything as it should be*.'

'He's here to blow the place up.'

Lewis dismissed this.

'You do know where you'll end up if we're booted?' Brass twirled his finger around his ear and cuckooed.

'What is this?' Lillian pushed into the circle. 'Who is making schemes in my kitchen?'

Snuffy explained Cass and the suspicions.

'Do you think this is the first time they have sent their little worms?' she said. 'You must trust in Teddy.'

'It's me,' West said, stepping back against the cooker. 'That's why he's here, why they're checking up.'

'It is not, my sweet,' she said.

They watched West leave, only surfacing from their inaction when Lillian barked. 'Wretches. Find my beloved West. My love today is only for him.'

On their way back Cass, with Teddy talking at his side, walked through the group and this had the effect of dispersing it into the corners of the building. It was Teddy's nervousness rather than any ferocity on Cass's part that was unsettling.

Radford found himself in his room, the door shut, *An Account of the English Civil Wars* bringing itself to attention. He felt again for the tiny ripples of its cover and traced *t-h-e-E-n-g-l-i-s-h*. It smelt older even than it looked, like the pages might be in decay.

He thought of nothing that could ease West's mind. What he'd said was likely true. However invisibly, the house was connected to the outer cosmos, the secondary world, and West had tugged on the line. Radford was losing his talent for retreat. What did that leave him with? Worry. Worry and delusion, and the never-ending squabble between them.

He returned the book to rest.

FIVE

They spent the morning in the Long East Room conducting what had become a regular tryst. Manny would arrive first, laying out his cases, arranging tools and components, and he would be in the final stages of neatening as Radford rounded the corner.

He would pull up his chair: close enough that he could muck in, far enough away that Manny wouldn't flinch; to the side such that neither of them felt under examination. Idle chat was skipped and instead they congressed in wire, charts and the course of that electricity.

The few necessary words were spoken considerately. Manny would talk of objects being connected in series or parallel, of melted lead, of hertz and watts and farads. Of current being resisted and alternated. Radford would nod, add his affirmations of understanding or shake his head. Manny would begin again, holding a capacitor or battery at a new angle, or instructing Radford on where the hot iron should be directed.

Circuits were made. Their mornings dealt in mercury, silver and porcelain. Radford fell for the simplicity and difficulty of it all: there was so much to learn and for the first time this was something both frustrating and tempting. He wanted to know these things, how they came together.

Ohm's law. This was, Manny made clear, at the heart of the matter. Current equalled voltage over resistance. Current was *I*, voltage was *V* and resistance was *R*; *I* equalled *V* over *R*. Radford frowned as the brick wall of mathematics presented itself, but Manny told him to close his eyes and picture a hot, empty plain. Into this scene walked an Indian, feathered headdress and all, and he looked to the distance where a vulture was flying high above a rabbit. Could Radford see this? He could. He sniffed the dry air and heard the cries of the patient bird and the rabbit's fearful squeaks. The Indian was *I* then, and the vulture *V* and the rabbit *R*. So *I* equalled *V* over *R*.

A flash of recall came, of school. Radford had finished there only recently but it was already such a distant idea. The years, those who peopled it, already fog. As he strained to hold the sensation, a corrupted memory came, of life in a glasshouse. Humidity and heat rising as the day brightened overhead, his breathing becoming a difficulty though all the others chuckled on, untroubled.

He and Manny were close to done for that morning when Cass arrived. His shoes biting into the floor echoed around the unfurnished room. Manny became nervous and lowered his chin, letting curls fall across his eyes, and this disturbance incensed Radford. He wanted this pale, nasty presence gone from their peaceful shire.

But Radford nodded politely, saying, 'Good morning.'

'Just *good morning*, is it?'

'Good morning, Dr Cass.'

'Doesn't take much, does it?'

Radford imagined grabbing Cass's arm and twisting it behind his back, marching the pig out of the house and down into the filth.

'No,' he said. 'Doesn't take much.'

The doctor peered over the table. 'Do not allow me to halt your lesson, Mister …?'

He waited for Manny's introduction. As time burnt away and Manny, if anything, lowered his gaze further still, Cass's expression grew less tolerant.

'It's Manny, Dr Cass,' Radford said.

'Mr Manny.' Cass tilted his head, trying to make eye contact. 'Or is it Dr Manny? *Professor?*'

He spoke this last word with unshielded condescension. In his mind Radford gave the pig Cass a rough kicking while he lay helpless in the slush. He could remember no time when he had wanted so badly to raze another human being.

'It's just Manny.'

'Radford, isn't it?'

'Yes, Dr Cass.'

'I will not turn a blind eye to the boorish habit of misaddressing your superiors.' He waited, as if for confession or concession. 'I insist on remedy to this practice. So it will not be *just Manny.*'

Radford faced his friend, who was now beginning to pack away the table, his brow still bowed. He wanted Manny to be carried away from here, to be comforted and praised and built a palace of ideally conducting gold.

'So which is it? What is your title?' Cass was speaking now as if to someone hard of hearing. 'Shall it be Mister or Doctor or Professor? Because it can no longer be *just Manny*. No longer, sir. If this facility is to be rescued, and I say that it is, it will begin with the fundamentals of respect. So which is it to be – Pastor? Prime Minister? You must have qualifications. To what level are you qualified? Even this facility must require some level of competence from its staff. To what degree have you been awarded? Because *just Manny* is not going to be enough.'

'God damn, stop it!' Radford stood and sent his chair screeching back along the floor. 'Leave him alone, will you? Why are you doing this – why are you here?'

Cass's shock turned promptly to rage. He leant in until his face was an inch away, as if baiting for a reaction, then swung his open hand and struck Radford hard on the side of his head. Radford howled and clutched at his ear. It was hot and throbbing and he could now hear a frightening ring.

'You will show respect.' Cass threw looks between the two of them. 'Remember this.'

Through the pain Radford straightened his back and stood as high as he was able. He returned Cass's stare, adding a smile.

'Yes, Dr Cass. I will do my best.'

The man stormed from the room and it was some time before the gunshot of his footfalls retreated into quiet. The stinging in Radford's ear dimmed to a pulsing headache as he helped to pack away the table.

When only a few containers of components remained, Manny pushed his hair back and said, 'I'm sorry.'

'Don't worry about it, Manny.'

'Are you okay?'

'Yes.'

The desk was clear and all else was zipped and clipped tight.

'I am, sorry,' Manny said again.

'Don't be, please. It's that son of a bitch.' Radford raised his palms. 'Sorry.'

'No, he is a son of a bitch. As far as I can tell.'

They exchanged a chuckle and Radford was consumed by the impulse to take Manny into a hug. He moved towards the man but realised his error, instead thrusting out his hand for an awkward handshake.

'Just tell Cass the truth next time, will you?' Radford said, playing weakly. 'Tell him your title, Lord Admiral.'

Manny smiled but his face withdrew into bashful plainness. The lesson over, Radford went as he always did, pausing at the room's exit to give a cursory wave, the pair parting in wordless satisfaction. He began his search through the rooms, though now distracted by his ear; the thing was foreign and hostile, beating against his skull to the rhythm of a heart.

The atmosphere had become primed with fractious energy since Cass's boarding and the doctor's presence had prompted a great show of things being done. Boys feigned obligation to some task or lesson, moving needlessly between rooms in an attempt to cast the Manor as a place of occupation. Yet Cass induced in them a faltering nervousness that ruined the possibility of anything like work.

Teddy alone was immune to the doctor's stultifying effect. It was true that he had been uneasy when Cass arrived, but now it was as if he had taken a decision to show the house at its most unapologetic.

When Lewis and two other boys had traded vicious punches one morning Teddy had brought it to a swift conclusion, separating the three from the dozen others assembled, but made a point of letting the incident pass without retribution. West had recounted this to Radford later in the day; with the tussle ended all had watched for Cass's reaction. In the commotion the doctor had struck his head against a doorframe: he had taken to trailing Teddy like an aggressive shadow, so when Teddy lunged to break Lewis apart from his combat the doctor had jumped back into his injury. West beamed as he described the radishing of the doctor's face: Cass's sourness at Teddy's failure to discipline.

While Teddy had become more cavalier, Cass had begun to show a disquieting restraint. Until then it had been a parade of blustering and thrust fingers, but now the fury remained corked. Radford wondered if this was some new strategy and discussed his worry with West, that Cass could be appeasing rage with the knowledge that each deficiency would be added to a list and this catalogue would constitute the Manor's warrant. West thought that this point may have already been passed and Cass was in fact delighting from a verdict on the fate of the house, each failing only more dirt on their grave.

It was thus a surprise when Radford heard Cass explode one morning.

'Vermin!' he brayed in his most outrageous command voice. 'We are with mice!'

The animals' presence was well known to the house. They were regularly seen queuing along skirting boards as the dining room emptied, but their company was accepted as no more strange or harmful than any other. Cass, however, demanded action.

It was an accidental alliance, with Cass's disgust and the boys' boredom and unhealthy lusts finding a common outlet. Several hours were spent laying traps throughout the buildings and great pleasure was taken – most obviously by Rich – in the devising of bait. Meat rinds were made sticky and tied with cotton. Kitchen scraps were ground to stinking pastes and applied. For nothing but cartoon amusement the boys imagined setting traps with cubes of yellow cheese, but the pantry's slender wedge of cheddar was deemed too precious. Radford only watched, this being no sport.

An afternoon. Seconds after the clearing of midday dinner, Radford and his faction were out and away. It had been agreed on during the late morning. Cass could not be abided any longer so, if he was resolute in staying, it was they who would have to quit the house, if only for a stretch of hours. They would depart for the cemetery, another wake.

Another cavalcade of cigarettes, booze.

These same words and their actions, repeated and enacted again and again until they lost meaning: boys – smokes – snow – grog. The house now stood in the shadow of West's wound. So quickly had all become tedious, intolerable.

Half a bottle was in their possession and it would have to do. The attraction of mere escape was enough for Radford and the limitations on drunkenness meant an unpunished return. Brass made the suggestion of a genuine clubbing on Cass. Proper violence. They despised the doctor but above all they wanted to leave Teddy untroubled so the proposition was retracted.

Lips still warm from shepherd's pie they waited for their chance at the kitchen door and rushed across the grounds, through the break in the wall and into the white. They collected Snuffy and Victoria as they passed the coop, the pair having been in watch behind its far wall. On seeing Victoria, Radford grinned idiotically.

'Afternoon,' he said. 'Good afternoon, that is. Not that anyone says *bad afternoon*, do they? Even if they hated someone enough to wish that. I don't hate you, of course.'

In desperation to silence himself he ducked his head just as West leapt to avoid the edge of a bramble bush and the two of them collided. Luck and shouting kept them upright.

'Good afternoon,' Victoria said, nodding cordially. 'I don't hate you either.'

The snow had hardened so the group gathered pace. It was when they crested the long second hill that Radford first took notice of the yellow light hailing down and it brought him to a full stop. Like a grandfather on his first dawn of retirement he raised his hands to his hips, surveyed the land, its sunshine, and took in a chest-spreading inhalation.

It had been a condensation of circumstances: West falling away from Radford's side and Snuffy wandering ahead with Rich. So Radford was walking with Victoria and finding himself asking all the questions he despised.

'Which was your school?' was his final and worst.

'Ooh, one of the terrible ones,' she answered. 'So terrible that the typing school wouldn't take me after. Equipped with entirely the wrong attitude, it turns out. Honestly, Radford, what kind of school doesn't prepare a girl's attitude for typing?'

A silence came between them and Radford found his heart slowing, his lungs slackening. Victoria shoved him in the ribs.

'You seem altogether too peaceful,' she said. 'Thought you were all head-cases?'

'Not all of us. Some just have the wrong attitude.'

Her laughter thickened into a snort. She watched the others ahead and Radford noted West now fifty feet behind. She talked of news from home and the trains becoming stuck just out of London, and he talked of his uncle and his worry of being caught on the highway.

'Your uncle brought you?'

'Yes, I'd been living with him.'

'Ooh, and me with mine,' Victoria said. 'And he's on his own, is he, the uncle?'

He nodded.

'Fabulous, aren't they? Single uncles. They're the family you want when the family you have goes wrong.'

Radford gave the due smile and looked for the sun. It wasn't at all warm – in fact it seemed colder now than at any point since the Freeze had begun – but its glow was tempting and offered no suggestion of future ill.

She took his arm. 'Radford, if I ask you some questions, will you answer right away?'

'Okay.'

'I mean right away, without thinking.'

'Yes.'

'I knew you would. Goodie. So, which way is north?'

He wavered before pointing a finger straight up.

'Who loves you most?'

'Dog, I imagine. Forgotten his name.'

Her squeal was such that the boys ahead turned to face them. 'And what's the worst colour?'

'White,' he said without hesitation, kicking the snow and vanishing behind its wave.

They had come again into Winter's house. It watched down on this little train of trespassers who would repeat the same actions, speak the same words, as if they could conquer anything as undeniable as the season. They would stand over the graves of their own kind and tell their make-believe stories, taking to a numb and untouchable land by all their narcotics. And always setting their pathetic fires as if they held any power against the cold.

The birds were sent to listen in, to confirm the evil of these humans.

It could be different. They could accept Winter as they accepted its siblings, but instead they waged war. If this sad and branded group could not be its friends then what hope was there for the rest?

The winged spies reported back and it was just as always. Boys – smokes – revenge – grog.

Winter drew air into its cheeks and readied its spears.

Headstones were visible only by a few stoic inches poking through the surface and at the cemetery's far end its ground fell to become all unbroken wasteland.

Rich had been the one to explain the business of the wakes to Victoria and she had thought the idea a morbid one. Death – even these remote examples of it – was something that she couldn't make a game. The boys, she said, were welcome to it. Brass called out for the bottle.

'Not yet,' Rich said, getting in a bother. 'We have to choose.'

Brass demounted his marble cross and took the whisky.

'Please,' Rich said, going from stone to stone, brushing their faces. 'Done her. Done. Oh wait, please.'

Radford took his place with the others, assuming the positions he already knew so well. He readied his hands and lips for their parts and wondered how things could be any different.

The wake began with Lewis at the helm, having found the tomb of a man named Lewis. It was poetic or mundane. All the recurrences. Brass drinking first and declaring all the formalities unnecessary, Rich wanting all the ceremonies observed. Smokes and smokes. Bottles of copper. Even Victoria's patient distance, something new, seemed tired. The story of Lewis, a winner of the race underground, was a ludicrous one of a man fleeing to America to find oil and pearls and ultimately death by sex.

'A salute, then.'

And there was a salute, West a row back from the others, pushing into a tree's trunk while the living Lewis bowed, keeping his cigarette to his lips.

Who had made the choices that put them out on this island? The horizon was shortening in each direction, bringing mist in place of hills and treetops. What may once have seemed the great expanse of nature had gone the way of the house's novelty. Instead it was an incredible crowding, putting all in the foreground, in the short term. Radford wanted to see something of a world outside. Suddenly he cared.

Brass led the walk away, no-one offered a call to stay and soon they were marching across the hill back through their footsteps. With the last of the whisky drained, the mood quickened if not lifted. Lewis started up his snowballing and Brass amused himself by getting Rich on the back of the neck with a long stick. Radford repeated his grandfatherly gestures to the remnants of the sun, wishing for its return through the low heaven. As he stood tall, West approached, the last in the family line. They smiled, Radford more so, and began the walk.

After some consideration Radford said nothing. Twenty minutes went by, then thirty. They came to the thin river, now all grey concrete. Victoria had looked back at them at least a dozen times and signalled for them to hurry ahead. Each time Radford had returned a wave and West had kept his head down.

The river should have been beautiful, despite everything. The snow-loaded trees on its bank leant over its solid illusion and light caught in what remained of frosted reeds. They passed a small stone bridge that belonged in a children's tale.

'It doesn't matter,' Radford said, his plan collapsing; he resolved now not to bear West's silence.

They continued to walk for some time before the reply came. 'It matters that I've caused trouble.'

'You're exactly wrong.' Radford stopped them. 'You have brought trouble – that's the truth of it. You had a go at cutting out your guts and so they've sent Cass.'

'And that's trouble.'

They faced one another, Radford wanting to shake West to pieces. 'What's wrong with that?' Radford asked. 'I'm beginning to think trouble's at the heart of anything worthwhile.'

West's eyes were pink and shining.

'So it does not matter.' Radford took a laboured breath, trying to slow. 'Not to Teddy, nor me. What matters is you sticking a knife in yourself, and not because it might bring bother. We want you to be around and that's all. I require you, sound, and I don't think that's the first time I've told you. I need you altogether.'

They remained, quite still, buried to their knees. West began to dissolve, first at the waist, and though Radford held him by the shoulders he couldn't be stopped from sinking. West's mouth held open like a brute animal in a trap and Radford let this go on. He let it spill from West until it slowed of its own account and his lips were able to close. They helped each other back to standing.

'One of these dummies would give a speech at your wake,' Radford said, pointing ahead and starting them off home. 'That's reason enough to outlive this place.'

As they went Radford thought he could recognise his friend returning to West's features.

They were so confused, these humans. And so confusing. If they would only accept the cold in action as they did in words. A peace could bloom between them and perhaps a lesson could go untaught. Winter's hands could remain clean of blood.

Back at the house all went rotten. The group reassembled at the chickens and decided on a straight dash to Snuffy's. They could put on a record and piece together some cigarettes, enough to cover half an hour of them making the way back into the afternoon in unobtrusive pairs. All would be easy, but when they reached the room they found the door ajar and Cass waiting. Each pair fell silent and statuesque as the doctor became real. He waited for the last.

'That's all?' Cass retrieved the empty bottle from one of their hands.

Rich stormed. 'Christ, Lewis, what did you bring that back for?'

Cass pointed between Rich's eyes, silencing him. Lewis shrugged and began to mouth a rebuttal when the doctor caught sight. Allowing no time to pass, no possibility of ambiguity,

Cass struck Rich hard and the boy went down noiselessly. Brass took a knee and put out his hand.

'Stand,' Cass said.

He took Brass by the collar and pulled him upright. The boy braced himself for the strike but the doctor only put his fingers to Brass's chest and pushed him delicately against the near wall.

'Will it be now?' Cass asked, soft and drowsy. 'This free ride will end for you all.' He drew a circle in the air. 'That can be right now if you wish. Do not doubt me.'

Rich righted himself with his fist over his ear, shrinking while Cass grew in energy. The doctor's eyes swung slow and powerful as searchlights to Radford, Snuffy, settling finally on Victoria.

'What kind of girl are you? House cat, pet?'

'No,' she said, facing a reddening Snuffy and urging him to ease.

'But you're an animal, that's clear. What kind?' Cass kept on. 'A loyal kind?'

She hugged Snuffy to restrain him.

'Hand,' Cass asked of Victoria.

She looked into him with a resolve that seemed a declaration. He could do this, and she would not please him with the show he longed for.

'Hand,' he repeated.

In her movement Radford realised that around him were nothing but frightened children. He had allowed these boys to ripen in his estimation, to grow to giants, but here they were reduced to true form. Minor youth, no better than himself, with their mouths muzzled and heads bowed to deny each other.

Victoria alone was mighty. She would give the doctor not an inch of her true self and she would not run. She did not allow her gaze to drop from him as she raised her hand.

He took her outside by the wrist.

The boys came after, Snuffy losing himself among them, finding courage now to meekly protest from yards behind. She pleaded for them to stay quiet as she was pulled across the mush and into the house. She let out a yelp of pain as they crossed the threshold but began to laugh at Cass as he grew ever more angered and hurried. She raised a single, slowing finger to the trailing party.

They were to let this happen and Radford obliged, as did every last one of them. Each pitiful example. A man imagined he injured a woman, a woman defied a man; infants watched on. Cass took her to Teddy and outside his rooms she shouted for the boys to leave. The door was closed, opening briefly a few minutes later for Teddy to insist that all would be fixed.

She left that evening, taken to town by Teddy and Manny, the men returning the following day. Teddy spoke only to Snuffy and he in turn refused to report any clue to her fate. After a day the boys stopped asking and after a week they didn't speak of Victoria even among themselves.

Radford would slip away to the belfry when confident his absence would not be recognised. He insisted on this solitude yet drew no comfort from it. Introspection was no bravery. He was just a child standing alone, slowly freezing to nothing on the remains of dashed thrones and looking up at a barren sky.

The carrying-on of things.

*

The flicker of amusement in Teddy's expression grew as each minute expired and the complaints and petitions for explanation mounted. Teddy had them waiting for breakfast, having been standing on a chair by the fire for ten minutes, directing them to gather as they wandered in for feeding.

Before this, Radford had listened in to talk of the mouse traps. Every night they had been set and each morning they had been found empty. All had been triggered, their prize escaped. So it was a question of the stickiness of the baits rather than their appeal. Some suggested the use of more cotton and Radford even found himself supporting the idea of chewed toffees.

'You horrors, come,' Teddy said, high.

'He's had one of his ideas.' Brass rubbed his thumbs into his eyes. 'I'm going back to bed.'

Rich stood. 'Me too. Lewis, fetch me when grub's up.'

'No chance.'

Rich slapped his hands on the table. 'You don't appreciate me at all, do you?'

Teddy caught sight of Brass's retreat and whistled for him; Brass spun and returned to his seat without breaking stride.

'My poor brood.' Teddy was in sermon and the room settled. 'Are we not sick of ourselves? Are we not entirely ill with the sight of each other's loathsome, ugly faces? I look in the mirror and I see something appalling. Seeing you all here today, I am likewise sickened.' He tilted his face to the ceiling. 'We need to stretch ourselves. Make some rushing air.'

He spoke as if expecting excitement, or at least agreement, but found only drawn, hungry faces.

'An excursion.' Teddy came down from the chair. 'I was taken to holiday at Porthmadog as a boy. For one week we were there and for one week it rained without intermission. Lagooned in our rented room, my brothers and I fought with such ferocity that on the final day my mother took us to the shore. Despite the impossible weather she paid for the hire of a sailboat, half rate, for one hour. She perched on a large rock and watched as the shipman set our sails and pushed us into the bay. It was without question the loneliest hour of my childhood. Death, by fist or by squall, came remarkably close for us on that wretched dinghy and we begged for our return to land. However, what I remember most clearly was my mother's face. The look of relief, oh, it was something heavenly.'

He was lost in the memory, his hands raised, eyes shut. He awakened and made commands for the household to move through to the front entrance and there he waited for the landing room to fill before opening the doors and leading them outside. Radford and his group had found themselves at the front and so as they pitched out onto the snow were among the first to see the ship.

The picture was absurd, even to imagine, but there it was, twenty feet up the drive with Manny bearing an expectant grin at its bow – an ancient, decaying but undeniable, boat. Great metal blades modelled on ice skates were attached at its front and beneath either end of a plank at the hull's rear. The boys rushed to circle the beast and Manny grew ever more proud. He slapped the ship's underside. Teddy was looked to for confirmation of the vision.

'A marvel,' he signalled.

Boys ran their hands down the pitted hull and inspected the support structures of the blades.

Teddy spoke low to West. 'Best someone tell Cass that we'll be out for the day. Find him, will you? He's sulking. Tell him we're off sailing.'

Hours were condemned to hauling the ship to its river. Manny had shod the blades with wide wooden slippers, the toes of which had been sanded to a curve in the hope of dissuading a downward trajectory, but it still took a lusty, constant effort to keep the vessel from diving for soil. Shifts were taken in groups of six, each member taking hold of a length of rope anchored to the hull. Others would run about the stern, pushing hard against it until either balance or endurance failed. It was slavish work, but was taken to with fevered relish. They fought to be next up dragging. Rope burnt their palms and shoulders and they fell into singing and the chanting of *heave, ho*. Manny marched ahead and directed around obstacles. When they became inevitably stuck there would be a general cry for *all in* and each would dash to get their hands beneath some part of the vessel. They would count to three, the ship would rise on their cries as if taking a wave's crest, and the party would be moving once more. Teddy followed, the tug at the tail of the fleet.

They were being rewarded with a dream and Radford promised himself not to ruin it with judgement. He thought of Victoria, of her expulsion, and of what the rest of them deserved. Surely not this, but then, what comes to the bad? Because they were all surely bad.

At their destination the mainsail was raised and the tired, glorious cheer that followed split the sky. Lewis and another of the tall ones were called up to set the rigging. Cords were pulled and mechanisms engaged and on the captain's command the ship was pushed to the centre of the river's frozen surface. The boom was swung out to position. Though the breeze was slight and swirling, it took on a magic potency and the canvas went immediately taut and filled out to a splendid belly. Radford had his hands against the hull as it began to move under its own power. The crowd of bodies dispersed to allow the boat's passage: without need of humans and their fussing, it cut its own future across the ice.

Celebrations followed alongside while onboard Lewis looked panicked. The other boy stood and thrust out his arms to receive his adulation until losing his footing and falling back over the bench into Manny's lap. They tangled in steering cables and while they argued and shouted the ship took a distinct turn to port. It ploughed at speed into the bank and sent the squad sprawling hard across the deck.

The greatness of the cheer that met this drew new fire from the shy daylight. The boat was pulled back to the river centre, readied, and two by two the boys took their turns aboard. Radford noticed Foster come from the riverside with a searching look. There seemed a brief gesture from him to West, in return West showed an approving hand, and it seemed that they would be next. There was something to this – Radford hesitated at the immature word, *secret*.

However, in the crowded moments that followed, a horde overtook the bank and West and Radford gripped the sleeves of each other's coats, finalising a pairing. The view clearing, Foster seemed to accept this, pausing alone at another emergence of sunshine.

Lillian arrived with hessian bags of wrapped sandwiches and bottles of thinned juice. Cass came with her, though walking a meaningful distance behind and looking miserable. They all broke to eat and Teddy told the ship's tale. Manny had come to him with the proposition a fortnight earlier, having been offered the wreck by Farmer Gall. The thing had been languishing beneath sheets against the back wall of a shearing shed for fifteen summers. It had been Gall's son's and it was a relief to reclaim the space. Snuffy had been assigned as assistant for the conversion and they had vowed silence on the project.

After the meal an impromptu gang formed to convince Lillian onto the boat. She accepted Manny's hand and assurances as he sat her on the centre seat. The sail slapped against a fresh gust and they launched, Manny standing high as the assured skipper while Lillian laughed and the household ran alongside waving their scarves. Radford lost sight of the vessel as it drove into the low sun.

He imagined Manny telling Lillian of the finer elements of his design, pointing to the arrangement of wooden struts supporting the rear blades and the cable and pulley system he had deemed to provide angle to the steering edge at the bow. Manny had repeated these particulars for each successive pair as they took their duty as crew.

Radford eyed Cass. The man sat, silent and ignored, watching these voyages from the riverbank, keeping far from Teddy and seeming to grow more angered with each wasted minute. The indolence of it all.

There was no attempt to hoist Teddy aboard and he showed no inclination. He seemed happiest watching from the shore and his eyes sparkled with a clarity Radford hadn't seen. This was, he understood, a gift both given and received.

Just a fragment of calm.

*

Brass addressed those gathered at the table. 'Watch it, the pig's got himself soaked,' he said. Cass had just put the elbow of his suit jacket into the remains of his beef and gravy with no sign of removing it.

It was night, enough hours after the river for their puckered skin to have returned warm and scarlet. Enough time for their bellies to have been filled with steaming pasties and for all their day clothes to have been hung across lines of rope Teddy had commanded between the roof beams of the dining hall. The fire rampaged within its stone confines, fantastic at being alive. The adults had come together and Teddy had insisted on rounds of sherry to combat the cold within.

Cass, who had remained sullen and soundless since the afternoon, took his first two glasses with blunt nods. On Lillian's instructions – she had been disallowed from leaving the table by Teddy on the grounds that she was a blessed creature of Arcadia, being owed too much already from this undeserving lot – boys had retrieved the house meal from the ovens and delivered it on thin wooden platters. Cass had reached furiously for his and over the course of several pastry crescents the man poured and downed his third, fourth, fifth and sixth sherries.

It was in pouring the seventh that Cass reached the bottom of Teddy's bottle and finally noticed his gravied elbow. He asked if there was more sherry – there was, and Teddy went to his rooms to retrieve it – and calmly dressed his jacket over the back of his seat, removing his tie and unclasping his top three shirt buttons.

'Soaked.' Brass brushed away a crumb and began to stroke a comb at his fringe.

Radford relaxed into the thought that he had worked this doctor out. He could be reduced to a cool and useful conclusion: Cass was a remnant of the time before the war. He was all the worst of his kind without any of the sweet eccentricity – and what was the purpose of a charmless cartoon? The years had left Cass living in a single dimension and all his moves were predictable ones, so it was no wonder that he was scared and without humour, for everything he understood was no longer wanted. There was little hope for the doctor and Radford thought it a sad thing.

Exactly like overtired children the house left its retirement too late; when its members submitted to fatigue they did so malevolently. They kept their shoulders down and eyelids at half-mast, as if hoping the journey to rooms would be forgotten with sleep's arrival.

The mantle clock showed just nine when West, Radford and Rich were the last of the boys in the room. Lillian had them draw the centre tables together and so the three of them faced the elders. Teddy was packing his pipe and had lost only a little of his serenity from the day. Manny was tired but sat straight with satisfaction while Lillian lay across three chairs with her head in his lap, her bare feet crossed and balanced on the table corner. In a low, throaty whisper she had been singing the same old-seeming song for twenty minutes. Cass had continued pouring sherry, scraping the bottle across the table.

'Quite a craft,' Cass said with surprising lucidity, to no-one in particular.

Lillian stopped her singing and it was Teddy who responded. 'What's that, Doctor?'

Cass fluttered and his lips began to pucker and smack like a newborn's. 'Quite a craft,' he said again, bringing his eyes to focus and offering his hands in a tumble.

'The ship?'

'Can't say I've seen a girl like her.'

'Quite a genius,' Lillian said.

This threw Manny into a flight of embarrassment. His body sank as was typical and he brought a fist over his mouth, but Lillian took the fist, opened it and kissed the meaty flesh of its palm. Radford looked about the table and treasured the sharing of pride. In the weak firelight these boys could have been brothers, Teddy their contented grandfather. Lillian could have been in some real way French.

'Curious, isn't it?' Cass refilled his glass, bringing the liquid to and beyond its rim. 'How skill, capability, finds itself in different ways in different types.'

He left this sentiment to hang with the laundry, seeming to fancy that his audience might regard it as a fine one. Teddy stiffened.

'So often,' Cass went on, 'a capability will find itself in a man to the exclusion of other sorts of intelligence. That is true, isn't it? That certain types, good or bad, attract certain competencies and repel their opposites.' He took a drink, nodding as if on the threshold of profundity. 'Those of the mind are so often useless in the hands. Am I mistaken, Doctor?'

'Do call me Teddy.' Radford could see the sharp edge of teeth holding down his lower lip. 'And yes, Dr Cass, you are mistaken.'

'Come now, Doctor. Don't you go limp on me, for goodness' sake. I include myself in this description. I am a man of cerebration, like you. This is fact. I have no trouble admitting that I would struggle to know how one might tighten a leaking join or make repairs to a broken step. It is not our way.' He swung his hand as if dismissing a mosquito. 'I wish you would admit to what you are. There is no shame in knowing one's self, indeed, there should be pride in it. We are men of the mind and as such we can surely admit to being dolts when it comes to basic labour. It is a question of types. You will admit there are types?'

'Cass, that is enough.'

The man took a drink, slowing, digging in. '*Doctor*.'

'*Doctor*, of course.' Teddy stood, stowing his pipe. 'And that, as I said, is enough.'

Cass studied Teddy's face before guzzling more and coughing up a toady grin. 'There is a disease in this place,' he said finally. 'Smelt it the day I arrived and felt sure the rogue appendage would be found. It is now clear to me, however, that this disease runs right to the core. As such it is hopeless. You can cut away a blighted segment of apple but when you break the thing open and find it black and noxious at its centre, well, there is nothing to be done. There is a weakness in this institution. It is a weakness of will and there is nothing to be done.'

'How dare you,' Lillian said, standing. 'Pig.' She turned to Teddy, her eyes bared.

He gestured for calm. 'As I said, enough.'

'Oh, for god's sake man, will you not agree with what you know to be true? I have said nothing that has not been proven true by countless generations. By civilisation itself. There are types. The world around us proves this. There are types of the mind, of the intellect, such as you and me – and I am happy to admit this generally precludes us from the realms of hammers and saws and such. Pots and pans,' he added, turning his thumb at Lillian.

'You can stay well clear of my realm of pots and pans.' She kept Manny's hand tight into her chest.

'You know this,' Cass continued at Teddy with a flattened timbre. 'You are just too far gone with disease to admit it. You have gone soft and that is why these boys will continue to be poor and uncured. You cannot admit to even a fundamental truth. That there are types like me, strong in the mind and unskilled in the hands. And there are types like our Manny, sacred Manny, who are strong with their hands—'

'Enough!' Teddy brought his fist down. 'I will not say it again.'

Radford rose and lunged. 'You lousy sod.' He groaned as West caught him by the arm and Rich stood to keep him back.

'Shut your mouth,' West said at Cass while trying to settle Radford.

'Boys.' Teddy raised his hands. 'Please.'

'Animals,' Cass said, having not moved from his place or lowered his glass. 'You have untrained animals here, Doctor. You cannot continue to be so unnerved. Though as I have said, I fear it is too late. This house is with plague.'

Silence came. Manny had his hands now crossed and holding his shoulders. The fire had become a small, red smouldering and the humidity that had all evening seemed balmy was now only the stinking fog of ruined coats. Teddy flared as he pushed out a slow lungful.

'Dr Cass. You will agree that your visit has come to the end of its usefulness. You have spent some decent time with us and I am sure you have secured all that you came for. I will take you to the village in the morning. Prepare for us to depart at seven. Please see that you are ready.' He lowered into his chair and retrieved his pipe. 'Boys, it is late. Get yourselves upstairs. Thank you, lads. Immediately, without debate.'

They did not turn back, though West gave Radford a nudge to his ribs and smiled when, as they reached the base of the stairs, they heard from the dining room the roar of Cass's tantrum, a log crack, and the splendid cry of one of Teddy's matches being struck to life.

SIX

In the lane beside the pub they waited, as Snuffy had instructed. From the darkness they watched figures scuttle down the high street and disappear into the beckoning glow of The Black Bear, where Snuffy had promised he would find a way for adventure. Some of the boys had borne the wait with greater resolve than others. Radford and West had spent the half-hour devising conversation to distract from the cold. Brass had stood impassive while Rich and Lewis had with increasing impatience resorted to argument and games written in the snow with sticks.

Snuffy appeared at the window. 'Come on then,' he called.

They formed a crouching line and kept behind like ducklings and when they made the pub's door Snuffy wailed at them to stand and be natural. Brass went ahead, accepting the challenge as the rest were less able, Rich and Lewis wrestling after their shoulders collided in the doorway. They drew the attention of every last patron in the pub's front room, but the bar itself was momentarily untended and so they made the distance to a cramped corner table. They were isolated from the rest of the place by a helpful accident of pillars and a heap of stacked chairs.

'Don't dare complain,' Snuffy said. 'I've talked Dawn into rolling out a new keg. So keep it together.'

'And you don't start up all strict,' Rich answered across the table.

Lewis flapped his elbows in something like the Twist. 'Yeah, what's the point if we can't make a little merry?'

Snuffy showed his hands as they all silently jigged in place. 'Okay, right, but can we give ourselves a chance of getting mildly leathered before we're chucked?'

Brass saluted, the rest copied, and Snuffy called for cash. They grumbled but ultimately formed a decent kitty. Snuffy went for the bar, taking the notes and instructing that the coins be left unmolested. The atmosphere grew strong with smoke and chatter. Radford breathed in the history of the room, ancient beer resurrected by the heat and movement of feet. He thought of the centuries of bad opinion enmeshed in the wood beams. The many who had rested and cursed time in this place. He thought it the most delicious climate – he thought of growing old.

It took three trips to the bar spaced judiciously over fifteen minutes for Snuffy to equip each at the table with a pint. By joint decree the first had to remain untouched until the arrival of the last, and with the ceremony of a bitten thumb they began. It seemed an instant memory and erased all of the tedium of their last journeys in the snow. Cass was gone and that was to be celebrated. They brought their jugs together, cheering and spilling foam into the unvarnished table and so this occasion joined the woodwork with all those of the past. Radford wondered if this might be euphoria. He drank, he hugged West and he hugged Rich. He tried for Brass but the boy slithered out of reach.

The night tumbled on giving no suggestion of its end. With various excuses they had crept away as soon as tea was done, and their absence could not go undetected for long. The noise of Gall's Humber would surely have been heard. None of them spoke of this, of what trouble would await them or might already be unfolding.

Radford's neck was loose by the finish of the first pint. Several later and he was floating high as conversation became all whoops and hollering. Lewis and Rich spent what seemed a full hour at some game that involved thumping fists on the table, the calling out of *ones* or *twos*, occasionally turning fists into pointed scissors, and even more occasionally one or the other claiming victory and downing their beers. Brass's mood was the brightest and most surprising. He was giggling so furiously from one of Rich's impromptu poems that tears ran from his eyes and mucus gushed at his nostrils. Cries went up at this. Later Rich returned from the lavatory with a broken lamp in his hands, swearing he had no idea how it had come about and that, anyway, no-one had seen.

Snuffy had gone another way, the worst of them. As payment for his risk he had taxed an amount equal to a pint for each round he brought from the bar. So he sank two for each of their singles and by the time of Rich's confession Snuffy had descended into belligerence. He had engaged in a monologue of aggression over Victoria and her leaving. He stormed at Cass, at Teddy, at himself. The table absorbed the torrent and offered consolation but he raged on and turned all the fury back on Victoria. Even through his insobriety Radford cringed at all these awful, untrue words: that she was a deserter, the maker of empty pacts; that she wasn't worth following.

The first they knew of the clash was a loud business from the front bar. Despite Snuffy's maudlin turn the boys had continued into a blissful party and none noticed him slip away. This shouting was no Friday ribaldry. It was of a pitch and character that silenced the table as one and Brass led their run in. In the now busy front room Snuffy was writhing like a worm as one man held back his arms and another delivered a punch hard to his eye. He took the blow like it never was.

The landlady, Dawn, moaned from behind the bar, 'Get it outside,' and threw a rag that wilted by the brawl's side.

Just as the boys arrived other men joined and the lot of them fell into a tussle. A man sported a bloodied nose, holding a dripping hand to his face while lashing into Snuffy's side with his boot. Arms pulled torsos apart while Dawn continued her song of *outside*. More aimless blows and the boys took Snuffy by the legs into the street. Brass and Lewis attempted to placate the angry faces, imploring for it to be over. As farewell a man spat a bloody pellet into Snuffy's hair and the door closed.

Lewis was furious, stalking back and forth as Snuffy found his feet and began to lurch back inside. They pushed him away and he fell awkwardly into the snow. After a minute's failed protestation he stayed down, his breathing becoming an ugly, liquid sound. Somewhere in their escape Radford had collected a thump to his neck and his Adam's apple stung. He looked for West and the two of them stared wide and frightened.

They gathered around Snuffy, who had brought ice up to his blood-streaked mouth.

'Better take it back to the house.'

'No,' Snuffy said as he was helped up, his face unpleasant and sore.

'All of us,' Brass said. 'Come on, get you back, Snuff. Sleep it off.'

'I said no.' He ran at Brass and struck him on the chin, and kept running, past the windows of the pub, the neighbouring shopfronts, before turning down the next unlit street. They called to him, Rich and Lewis chasing, but after several minutes they returned: he was lost.

'To the car, home then,' Brass said.

West became weak. 'We can't leave him.'

They searched for an hour. Having followed each near street to its full and hopeless darkness they conceded that Snuffy wasn't going to be stumbled upon. There was a suggestion to ask for help back at the pub but it was agreed this could only further stir trouble. They would go back to the Manor. Some thought Teddy should be alerted immediately. Others thought Snuffy more than capable, even in his state, of taking care of himself for the night. Radford could come to no decision. They began home.

West had Radford come with him to Teddy's door and the man answered in full dress, the clock showing three in the morning. He took the news with no sign of surprise and moved at once into action. Manny was woken and asked to ready while the boys were to gather in the dining room and see to its fire. He asked them to fix some food but Lillian arrived and insisted on seeing to the warming of mash and sausages. There was no word of reckoning.

Radford was ill. From the rough business, from the booze. He and the others tended to their meal without discussion while Lillian sat with them, needlessly reminding them to finish their supper. Just as Manny and Teddy were gathering to leave, the telephone could be heard ringing upstairs. Lewis dashed to answer it. There was only quiet for a time, then he came down.

'Teddy, they want to speak with you,' he said in the room's doorway.

By next morning all the house knew. The murmurings could be heard from the Long East Room, where Radford and the night boys had been quarantined since Teddy returned from the phone call. A policeman was coming to the house. Teddy had relayed this without raising his voice or looking any of them in the eye. They were to remain with Manny in the room and not one word was to be spoken.

The officer was not what Radford had expected. He was old, older than Teddy, and seemed for the most part bored by the scenario, with no hint of menace or interest in scaring anyone straight from any crooked path. Teddy spoke with him for twenty minutes before bringing him down. Others had to be shouted away as they stood by the door in the hopes of catching on.

'The inspector will ask you questions,' Teddy said. 'Answer him truthfully and without delay.'

Snuffy had found his way over the fence of a house. He had made his way into a bedroom through a closed but unlocked window. The father and son had woken. Snuffy was being transferred to a city hospital.

The boys could offer little news in return. They told the inspector times and movements, of the alley and the pub and the fruitless search. Of coming home. The officer closed his notepad, nodding to Teddy as he went into the hall and left by the front door, replacing his cap as he went.

Teddy sat for a time. He was restraining no foul emotion; he only waited. 'It has been a long night,' he said at last. 'Go about your days. Sleep in the afternoon. Eat.'

It was a gruesome morning with light coming in through the parted curtain and illustrating their greasy faces. Radford saw the knuckles of his hands were burnt.

West was standing by the window, the sunshine catching the dust in the air around him. 'Is Snuffy …? I mean, will he be okay?'

'Of course not,' Teddy said.

Footsteps multiplied in the hall and the door handle shook, Radford imagining a straining ear by the keyhole.

'No word leaves this room,' Teddy spoke in a whisper. 'No confirmations or denials. They will hear soon enough but it will not be from any of you. You will do that for me.' They nodded. 'We have let him down.'

*

Some days later Teddy came to the dining room dressed as a new man. He wore a suit, well cut and of a colour that hinted at purple, but he had kept his top shirt buttons undone and his shoes showed an obvious heel. In keeping with this mix of dishevelment and high style, his face was unshaven while his hair was teased into something like a wave. He was smiling in a mischievous, foreboding way. Radford got a thump to the knee from West.

'Cherubs.' Teddy pushed his palms together and waited. 'I have been worrying. This house takes from the village while returning nothing. You'll agree? I have let this condition develop, I admit, but now, while the land is feeling such hardship, we are to make small amends. We go to the village for food, for our deliveries and comforts, yet of late we have returned only strife.'

Applause.

'You celebrate too soon, young brutes. You will be putting on a show.' Teddy blazed as this sentence moved through the room. 'That is right, an entertainment. In this time of hardship we will repay the village with light feeling. This is where my former self joins us at the frontline. The younger version of the man you know as Teddy. He is many things – an actor, a treasure, a man of all performance. He will be whipping you into fit shape for his sins.' He joined heels and saluted. 'The show will be tomorrow evening. At six.'

There was general disbelief and particular anger.

'Six it is,' Teddy agreed. 'We have the hall beside the church. Vicar will let us in at first light. Fine room it is, fine enough for you lot. We will be inviting all the village, all willing. And what shape will the show take? The likes of which the audience has never encountered. Humour, music, sword-fighting, flights of rhetoric and abandon. A proper stew. I will stoke you, because fire lies unnourished in all your centres.'

Around him boys began to moan but Radford remained quiet in his confusion. Was this some joke or punishment?

'Sleep on that thought,' Teddy finished. 'Eat, dear Lil has slaved. You'll be attending?'

She stood at the hall entryway. 'To see my *enfants* tread the stage? Keep me from there, I dare you to try. You put on a show for me, my ducklings. See that you do.'

The adults vanished behind conversation. Meanwhile the room hummed with fearful promise.

After pudding Teddy had them draw up advertisements.

The Good Boys of Goodwin Manor
present an apology in the form of…
WINTER FROLICS
Laughter
Drama
Knees-up
FREE TO ALL

Manny rigged a long trailer to Gall's car and by nine next morning each last member of the household was delivered to the church. As the boys came along the gutter of the high street looking as if salvaged from battle, villagers in equal number scattered and gathered. At the hall they unfolded wooden chairs into rows, and the vicar departed after receiving repeated assurances that any and all damages would be paid for by the evening's end. Teddy had shaken the holy hand, insisting that he return at six for the show. The vicar had nodded vigorously and agreed to nothing.

Teddy stood over the edge of the small stage at the hall's end and cupped his hands. 'Gentlemen! Do keep your enthusiasms in check. Retain a little vim for the performance.'

He jumped off with not quite enough sprightliness and was only just saved by Lewis in a dexterous panic. The old man straightened and walked on, collecting Manny and Lillian and taking them to the door.

'Morning tea,' Lillian said, checking her collar. 'Scones with clotted cream if they have any.' She and Manny became silhouettes as they walked into the day's paleness.

When the chairs were done Teddy sat on the lip of the stage and waved them in. 'Come, come, come. Fellows. Can I ask you – what do you know of me as a young man?' All was quiet outside of some skittish murmuring. He pulled on his lapels. 'What do you imagine?'

Only Brass seemed ready to respond and Teddy cut this short before it left the boy's mouth. 'Before conscience and schooling had the better of me – before succumbing to the wretched bore you see in front of you – can you believe I had another life?' He began pacing the stage and held his palm to his heart. 'I am offended. You do not recognise me? For you see, I – I was an actor. All truth. I was an employee of *the arts*. I tell no lie. I pretended, in plays and whatnot, for cash money.

'I want to tell you a secret. May I trust that it goes no further? Thank you, boys. I do not know much, but there is a notion I have stumbled upon that I can verify as fact.' He lowered to a whisper. 'The acting never ends!' He spun in place. 'One simply becomes so well rehearsed the whole trick seems real. It never ends!'

He turned about, adopting increasingly ridiculous poses to increasingly rapturous applause. Radford wondered where the real Teddy had gone to, and what he intended by all this. He knew better of the man to think it all merely a distraction. A lesson, then? Teddy insisted this was never his impulse. So again, that question – to fall in or rebel? Perhaps the lesson was in how little it mattered either way.

They were split into a half-dozen huddles, given a folder of scripts, and each was presented with his part. It was during the examination of their piece that a scuffle flared from Radford's group. He had seen Foster break away from his assigned partners and come across the hall with unclear intent. It seemed to be no challenge, with the boy loitering benignly, but Brass demanded to know what he was doing in their company. Foster gave no reply and in return Brass charged at him.

They had each other by the cuffs. The great difference between the two came true, Foster twice the size. Others, now between them, had put hands to Foster's chest and compelled retreat while West started a defence that was consumed by protest. This was the opportunity for a display of courage, for a genuine correction: Radford could extend himself, to the attempt of a fix. He made not one movement and watched the boy remove himself.

Foster stood apart from them, with his arms wide. 'What can I do? Hey? What would you have me do?'

Brass drew a finger across his throat and Foster just watched this, his eyes dulled.

'All finished,' he said. 'I'm done.'

He lit a cigarette and crossed the room, strolling without further signal out the door. He seemed an angel and Radford was truly without character.

Having missed all this but for its noise, Teddy had come to them, now indicating calm and attempting a stained grin. 'I hope you're ready for something special,' he said. 'First though, two questions. Who's heard of George Formby? And who's going to wear the dress?'

They had been assigned a song, 'When I'm Cleaning Windows'. Radford had some memory of it: the story of a cleaner and all that he saw on his rounds. The boys would be acting out the tale. Formby played a ukulele or a banjo, Teddy couldn't be sure, but regardless they would have to make do with the hall's piano. Radford would have to make do. He again argued his inability but Teddy had already accepted the notion. West announced that he would assist, went to the instrument, and with a few stray lashings revealed his talent.

'I'm a quite excellent player,' he said and let loose a precise ascent of notes. 'I hate to play, but I'm quite excellent.'

'A-ha!' Teddy punched the air.

Lewis, it turned out, was the one to wear the dress.

Appeals came for dinner, for a break.

'Break?' Teddy ran between them, amazed. 'But there is so much that is still less than it could be. Less true. Desire will push you on. Keep the lion hungry, boys! Keep the lion hungry.'

*

Six o'clock came, with all the house cramped and crouched at the back of the stage. Radford was sicker than he would have believed bearable and his eardrums swelled to breaking with the chatter and whispered foretellings.

How quickly show time had come and with what pitiless momentum. After Teddy announced *one minute* something like terror possessed their souls. West was visibly expanding and contracting. Brass, even Brass, had a rivulet of sweat leading from his shining temple to his damp collar. Rich bobbed up from under the curtain.

'You should see it.' He scampered through, following a hail of shushes. 'They're all here.'

A platoon had been sent out to drum up an audience. They

had been made to neaten their hair, told to keep civil tongues in their mouths and to knock on each last door of the village. Radford had heard the reports of unenthused townsfolk and convinced himself that none would attend.

'Time, lions,' Teddy said.

He looked back at his actors as if seeking assurance and, receiving none, did the button of his jacket, launched a mayoral smile and strode ahead. The curtain went up: Rich had lied not an inch; the hall was brimming. The village met Teddy's entrance with polite applause but kept stony looks, their coats and scarves not yet removed.

'Blessed ladies, devoted gentlemen,' he cried, advancing such that he seemed almost to levitate past the edge of the stage. 'We come to you, humbled. We, lowly mice of the Manor, offer ourselves. We are without talent, we are without moral exception, we have not learnt our lines, but we are yours. Tonight, if you will have us, we are yours.'

Radford felt as if he were rising into the roof beams, yet was aware of the warmth of West's body through his shirt sleeves and of the near breath of anxious cattle. He saw the audience, the women and men, the dust, the church ghosts. He was lost, joyously.

The sporty boys were the first to go forward, arms linked, oscillating in time with a tune, scripts of diabolical vaudeville poorly secreted behind their backs. A group performed a scene from *Look Back in Anger*, a play that Teddy insisted would be adored by the village. It transpired that it was perhaps a little *modern* in style. The first great cheer arose during the juggling and magic, two acts combined at the eleventh hour. A billiard ball was lost towards the audience and plucked from flight by a round man in the second row. He kept it aloft and turned to the back of the hall, bowing to the applause before lobbing the red orb back at the stage, where it sent the magician and his bowler hat to the floor in one thrilling motion.

Radford's group was next. Into the silence the piano seat creaked a high note. West gave Radford an elbow, then Teddy a nod, who in reply completed his onstage bow and went to the boys and darkness at the back of the stage. Their song began and Radford rose again to the timber of the ceiling. The smell of sawdust, of the wood's ancient construction. The saw's teeth marks like mountains across the grain.

West had taught him a trio of chords, so it was Radford who began by banging three fingers against three white keys while West did the rest. Lewis drew the first laughter, centre stage, a blonde starlet on a cushioned chair. He pursed his lips, he checked the springs of his wig. He exposed a pale neck to boys who ran around in a series of imprecise but gutsy mimes. Teddy sang from the rear of stage, of the window cleaner and his spying.

Radford felt West's ribs meshing against his own as they leant into each other. As the fourth verse came to its end, he realised that no concrete plan had been reached as to how and when the song would cease, and turned to West. It was then that the first of the apples struck: it hit West at the base of his neck and exploded in a pathetic way across the keys. Lewis took one in the chest and let out a hurt sigh. Brass ducked as a green-red blur shot by his ear but stepped into the path of one flying low and flat and he barked as it broke apart on his knee.

Foster, by the front row, was taking apples from a box at his feet. The piano took another hit, square on, making it ring as a funeral bell, and West put his hands up in defence of Radford. Foster's face was warped with anger while dumbly he continued the attack. Adult voices called for him to be stopped and some seated close moved towards him but then away in uncertainty. Foster's size menaced them, the hulk. House boys came running, dragging him into the darkness of the side wall. The apple box turned over and its remaining munitions rolled away between ankles. Radford saw the dimly lit swinging of punches.

Teddy's voice rose louder than the rest. He had his arms around the actors, keeping them from the affray and directing them back to the stage. He cried again, 'No!', making it clear that they were not to stop, that it *could not stop*. 'It goes on.' His finger thrust in the piano's direction.

West looked in pain at what was being done to Foster. Radford could imagine nothing to bring either peace so he started again at his chords. He thought of his first evening at the Manor and its humiliation, of standing alone in the belfry later that night. What had it all been for? He went on striking his small family of notes and urged West to stand and to play, speaking only for his partner's ear.

Slowly, West rose with him and continued, the tune scoring Foster's bundling outside and the closing of the door. A man leant hard against it as the audience resumed their places. Lewis too reclaimed his seat and straightened his wig as Teddy hid again.

The tune played, Radford anchored now to his role, and so some small triumph was declared. The story began again of this window cleaner. Lewis re-puckered his lips. Stiff with nerves the mime recommenced. Some whistles joined the clapping of the woman in the front row and it went on. West, now in tears, played his part.

*

Their bodies warmed around hot orange barleys. The dining-room fire was in absurd spirits as talk rioted among the dancing and re-enactments. Music came loud from the radio. Teddy stood on a table mimicking the jugglers, the comedians, Lewis with his hands pinched round his swaying hips. They cheered the memory and Teddy leapt to the floor to deliver more slaps on backs, more congratulations.

He had seen nothing like it, and he had seen Olivier's Richard III. He had seen Gielgud at the Haymarket, and still, *nothing like it*.

'As angels would be in heaven. As the stars must shine to make themselves seen to the night.' He was up again. 'As it must have been to stand inside the universe in the flames of its creation.'

It went on for hours, well after all had been returned from the village. Foster had been in the last bunch, surprising all – according to Lewis he had escaped upstairs. Radford wished he had seen what state he'd been left in, how hurt. Who was attending to Foster, and where had it all come from? West too was missing. The house celebrated and Radford was ashamed.

*

Much later, with the excitement dissipated, Radford went to his room with the desire for dreamless slumber. He had begun to undress when the tapping came to his door. It was Lewis and Brass, the two of them peering down the hallway before letting themselves in.

'We're getting Foster,' Brass said in a sharp whisper.

'What do you mean?'

'*Getting*.'

Radford saw the rolling pin in Brass's hand and another in Lewis's.

'He's a pig, I am sick of it,' Brass said, twisting the pin fondly. 'That liar has made this place hell. You know he's due.'

'I don't know a thing,' Radford said. 'And if you're right, he'll get his in time. Leave it.'

'If we don't step up, nothing will be done. Teddy isn't going to lift a finger.'

'You can't. You'll be sent down for starters.' He saw Lewis's nervous resolve. 'Please. Please, leave him.'

'You're a part of this.'

'You'll be locked up.' Radford scanned hopelessly between them. 'Lewis? Locked up, properly.'

'We'll be sweet,' Brass said. 'You just get him out to the coop, Radford, that's all. No-one will know.'

'That's mad for a start, what's getting him outside?'

'Booze, fags – you go to him … it's a peace offering. You've got whisky and smokes stashed in the coop. He'll follow, you know he will.'

Something true and dark was behind this. Brass wanted to hurt Foster in a way that frightened Radford in its scale and familiarity.

'What is it between you?' he asked. 'It's not just tonight. You've always wanted him done in.'

'He ruins everything. You know he does.'

'He doesn't ruin a thing, he's never given the chance. And when has he been a liar?'

Brass flinched, and disguised it so quickly it almost ceased to be. Radford, though, saw the shadow of an injury.

'What has he done – has he lied about you?'

'You don't know what you're talking about.'

Lewis stood by through this, as if hearing nothing. He was victim to Brass's charm and convinced by it: Radford had been in that place.

'He's lied *to* you. Is that it?'

'Just do your part.'

Whatever crime Brass felt casualty to, it was something primitive, and Radford accepted that he would never know what shape it took.

'No,' Radford said and stood fast.

Brass grabbed at Lewis and left, sheathing his club as they travelled the hall.

Radford tried for sleep, door shut, light out, but could only watch the static grey canvas of the ceiling and the meagre contentment it offered.

'Pigs,' he said aloud.

He reached for the lamp and went to his hiding place to retrieve the flattened bag of tobacco and papers. He took matches from the drawer, pulled on an outfit and made the journey up the hall. He said West's name and gave several muted knocks before his friend's door opened beyond its permanent gap. He shook his bag at the darkness. West dressed and they went towards the belfry, not speaking until they reached its door, when West's eyes ripened into consciousness.

'I didn't know you were stashing,' he said.

'Enough for a couple.' Radford began to push against the thin wood. 'That dumb Brass. Damn him, he can't be helped. He's rotten-minded. Lewis too. Jesus.'

'Why?'

'Boiled my blood. This bloody door – Christ.'

'Here.' West added his weight to the effort. 'What did they do?'

'They've got some idea they going to batter Foster. Do him in with rolling pins. After everything, that's what they settle on.'

West took Radford by the wrist. 'What do you mean?'

'What it sounds like.' He saw a flash of temper in his friend's face. 'It's just talk. They wanted me to bait him outside. After everything. It's just talk.'

West's grip became painful. 'Bait him where?' he demanded.

'The coop. The coop – get off.' Radford thrust him away. 'What's this? It's just Brass and his talk, Lewis is only being dragged along. *West.*'

He spoke this last bleak syllable as near to shouting as he dared but West was already at the hall's end, throwing himself at the first of the stairs.

If that night's joy could be extinguished there was no hope for any other. Radford stood atop the two feet of snow hiding the belfry's floor, taking advantage of this uncommon height to view the scene. All this that summer must replace with a wide unbroken lawn. Trees that were no more than silver blades threatening against the blazing moon. Floodlit nothing beyond.

Foster had done a share of ruining that night. He had spoilt with his assault, but it was in the song's conquering of him that the dirty engine of the night had been fired. They had resisted and excluded, they had kept hungry, and so they had gone on. And now this mess intended by Brass. They could all be damned. Radford had his two smokes' worth of tobacco and they could not rob him of that. He pressed against the chalky stonework, breathed the deadly air and thought of the night that had slipped away. The smoke alone loved him and understood.

He was thinking already of the second stick when Foster, wrapped in a chequerboard quilt held tight at the neck, came trudging below with an unhealthy gait. Radford felt no anger, no impulse of aggression. He wanted to send Foster inside to the safety of the fire but no shouting came to his lips, just the sodden remains of an exhalation.

West appeared to the extreme left, pausing as he came into Radford's view. Now the world beneath seemed exactly as if it were a stage, West having taken his cue and come from the wings. Foster hadn't yet seen him. West hesitated twice and then – with not a scratch of misgiving – screamed out Foster's name in a voice made crazy by the wind. West followed towards Foster, who had stopped in fright before calling back for West to go to hell. West tried the name again, this time adding a softened plea, but Foster already had a blanketed fist raised when he faced West and began to run.

'No! No!' West shouted.

This cry was not for Foster, but for the two greyed figures by the Manor's west corner. Brass and Lewis were steaming in with clubs raised, just as they said they would. Radford's cigarette smouldered between his fingers and he flung the glowing stub into the air as the battle reached Foster. Brass stung him on the chest as Lewis followed with a pin to his knee. The hooded aggressors made no sound and Foster groaned as the wood struck his body, the blanket falling around his feet. It was West who wailed, *no*, over and over, until he could get himself between Foster and the violence.

'Move,' Brass commanded.

West lowered his hands to his side. 'No.'

'Move!'

Brass jabbed him hard in the stomach and West gave a whine as he fell. Lewis came all at once forward and delivered a gross blow to Foster's jaw. It was the noise of leather on willow, the divine and English sound, and Foster went down holding his head.

West stood again and thrust out his hands, making Lewis look to Brass for direction. Brass, shaking and heaving, lowered his club and directed the pair of them back to the house with a snap of his hair. He spat on Foster as they went by. They ran on and vanished.

West dropped to a knee and put his hand to Foster's still face.

It all happened too, too quickly.

Foster brought his own hand across to cover West's and like this Radford saw them as a bronze statue. For this shortest time their union was at peace. Their history. Love. Foster broke them free of it, pulling West into the ground and standing over him. He kicked West in the side, twice, three times. He wheezed with each blow and West raised a palm, seeming to beg.

It happened too quickly – faster than Radford could appreciate.

Foster took West's hand, yanked him to his feet and twisted his arm behind his back. West made no sound and Foster ran the two of them in a stumbling heap away from the house and against the trunk of one of the great, bare trees. Foster had him by the hair and pushed his face against the bark. They stood in a fishnet of sickly light and Radford saw Foster struggle against his clothes and West's limp, unfighting body.

Trees bore witness to so much. The passing of kings and centuries of wordless battles. They saw whole lives, their beginnings and vicious ends. And yet they did nothing. Said nothing.

Foster had ripped away West's belt and pulled down on the back of his trousers. He unbuttoned his own and they inched down his thighs as he began his savage thrusts. West made no calls at this frenzy against his body, no more pleas. Foster made babyish grunts and his pants continued to shake downwards until his movements ended. Until he was done, depleted.

Radford lost sight of the two boys and saw instead versions of himself. The half of him as he could be, hurt and so violent and destined for catastrophe; and the other, all frail light so easily eclipsed. One couldn't be both, surely, and yet it seemed beyond the realm of choice. One might have to win out against the other. One might have to kill.

Foster stood tall and released his grip on West's hair. He pulled up his trousers and walked towards the house at a canter that suggested nothing, exiting as West held himself in a hug around the tree.

West found his belt and replaced it, slowly fixing his clothes. He followed the others' path back to the house, leaving the stage bare. Just fake snow and a painted background. What remained with Radford must then be merely prop.

The thought rushing through him couldn't have been genuine because it wasn't anger or distress. It was the wrong thought. Radford was envious, of West and Foster having shared this thing. They had stepped ahead of him, and away.

Radford waited to be corrected. He slid his unlit cigarette into his pocket.

These creatures Winter saw, these loveless things.

They were so wretched and so familiar. How could they not see the common colour of their centres? All they did was hurt.

The following morning neither Teddy nor Foster would come to the dining room for breakfast. West came and ate as normal, somewhat quietly but otherwise as usual. Lewis and Brass continued unaltered; the attacks were not discussed. Teddy would not be seen at the Manor for three full days. Foster was gone too, but his vanishing was complete, his few possessions cleared from his room.

SEVEN

The storms had departed but left a cold all the mightier. It came with no battering and fewer screams, and the impression formed that this might just be the new way of things.

Foster's disappearance was not lingered upon. Boys had fled before, Radford was assured. It was to be expected. That was what children did; they ran.

West continued to announce the newspapers. The last of the blizzards had persisted for a day and a half and left parts of the country in drifts reaching twenty feet. More regular deaths, more strandings. Hitting harder for many, football fixtures had ground to a near stop. The third round of the FA Cup seemed like it might never be allowed to end, with its games postponed again and again. The pitches were either buried or had turned to mud and the boys knelt at the radio for results that would not come. Radford stood by West for his readings but recognised fatigue in these same old words. Like West he was numb to the talk of the Freeze and its supposed power.

He took to spending time in the sparse garden at the rear of the house, with the unvisited coop in sight and the belfry keeping watch from high above. As he wandered the ground he made paths between trunks, inspecting the bends of roots as they dived under the earth for shelter, taking his hands from his gloves and exposing them to the stone of the trees' flesh. It was too much inside the house. Too much chatter on football and rock-and-roll and everything else a thousand miles away, other people's lives. Too much silence on anything that mattered, not that he knew what that might be. Inside seemed to hold nothing but excuses. The trees, at least, offered none of these.

He went out in the snow because he wanted to understand. He returned each day to the exact tree that had stood victim to West's hug and the shoving of his face against its bark. Radford pushed his own cheek against the surface, wondering if he might be told some secret. He heard nothing of consequence, just a quiet beach's shore, a more distant one than those trapped in seashells.

In this new spirit of honesty he admitted that he hoped West would find him out there and bring answers. It would be so neat: West would spill on the matter and he would be no longer left behind. In the regular world, Radford had in fact seen much less of his friend. Partly for all the hours he was spending under the trees, partly for West's distance. He was keeping alone, at times planting himself in an armchair close to the fire for all of a day. A few times Radford had seen Lillian instructing him to pull further away from the heat. When West and he spoke it was not strained: it was disastrously usual.

That day Radford had spent all the time since dinner

outside and it was late afternoon when Teddy came into view, his hands clasped behind his back, eyes up.

'Radford, child.'

He nodded, having pushed himself away from a tree to standing. 'Teddy, afternoon.'

'Not much of it left, not much.'

Teddy continued strolling and Radford jogged until he was level, noticing that Manny was twenty yards behind doing a bad job as a trailing spy.

'Have you been out a little?' Teddy asked.

It occurred to Radford that, unlike all the others, Teddy never asked questions he knew the answers to. 'Yes, a little.'

'Not me, been inside for too long. Far too long without realising. Think I'll go for a tramp out to the starlings' roost. See if I can't catch them flocking as the sun leaves.'

'Where's that?'

Teddy stopped. 'No-one has taken you to the starlings?' He took Radford's hand and called over his shoulder, 'Manny, hurry along. We're for the starlings.'

It was indeed a proper old tramp, up several long hills and down into the seat of as many saddles. They kept to firm ground as much as was possible but were forced through drifts and soft pockets. Teddy grew in energy with each obstacle, huffing in a pleased way and digging on with a stick that he had picked up early in the journey. Manny had given up on his surreptitious distance, whatever its purpose had been, and walked with Radford.

They reached a bare thicket and Teddy had them stop at its edge. He pointed ahead with the stick at a broad row of trees and Radford could now see the shapes that clung to their branches. The starlings appeared like black leaves. So many that numbers seemed not up to the job.

'Friends,' Teddy said.

Radford stepped out to take in the full sight of the roost. It went on for what looked like a mile, though it couldn't be that far. A great row of what Manny explained were maples. Straight as a good fence they grew between two fields, one flat and the other sloping down and away, and together the trees occupied a tremendous space of sky. Fifty feet high at least, they hung as the skeletons of clouds, just overlapping, the ends of their slender branches touching. The crunch of their walking having stopped, Radford heard the talk of infinite animals. It existed as a single note and though shrill as an alarm he found it a pleasant thing.

'Can we go closer?'

'Of course,' Teddy said, looking flushed and fatigued. Manny kept a slow pace with him and a body's length behind.

'They won't be startled?' Radford asked.

'Why would they be?'

They went closer until everything above and before them was only stick and bird. The sound was incredible. Radford found himself beginning to laugh in the union of nerves and appreciation. He kept turning back to Teddy for permission, like a toddler approaching a beach's waterline. Teddy swung his stick onwards.

'They may treat us to a show,' he said.

The three of them stayed twenty yards from the first of the line. Every inch of branch was occupied with the hunched figure of a starling. They chatted and fidgeted, swapping place for place. One would jump off, flying in a livid arc, only to return to its launch site. The animals found topics for a million sermons while preparing to bed down. The humans found no reason to speak or grow tired, while behind its cloud the sun was dipping entirely out of use.

They waited.

'Been hearing things in the wash-up from Cass and his report,' Teddy said. Radford couldn't be sure whom the man was speaking to. 'They're having ideas,' Teddy went on, looking to the birds. 'They do this, come with their proposals. Always on the topic of severity, of discipline, can you believe it? We're forever accused. Always too brutal or too coddling. That's the question, isn't it? What to do. Starve the cold or feed it. Anything less than total cure demands explanation.'

Teddy went quiet and the amber of the sky drained away. The starlings' show, whatever that was, never came.

It was left to Manny to raise the idea of returning. Lowering his eyes from the maples' heights Radford saw Teddy by the trunk of the near tree, poking into the snow with his stick.

'The cold,' Teddy said. 'All too cold.'

The bodies of dozens of starlings lay motionless in the powder. Teddy turned the ground over to reveal more buried beneath. Radford looked in the direction of the next trunk and saw that the dozens were actually hundreds. Corpses lay like dropped fruit beneath the canopies.

'This winter,' Teddy said. 'This rude nature, it's too great. I was taught to recognise the sublime – do you know about this? Ecstatic joy, they said. In the face of the unthinkable, the joy in knowing you're in a place of safety. You recognise the sublime. Well, what if you're not safe? What then, if you're not safe?'

Manny had moved to his side. As Radford came around he saw that Teddy had broken, the three of them a hopeless triangle. Teddy took no care to hide his sickness and was limp against Manny's arms. The old man was an abandoned nest.

They waited.

Light was truly failing and during a moment when Teddy seemed to be catching his breath Radford helped put him upright and they began their clumsy journey home. Radford took a final look at the great roost and at its fallen members beneath. They were entirely untroubled, not a feather displaced.

The walk back was difficult and slow and Teddy stopped several times in desperation. At one interval he pulled Radford close. 'You will hear so much advice. You will be told all the things you must do, that your character must develop. I say no. I say set those ideas into the fire. Stay blank if that's what you are. Existing can be enough. They will tell you otherwise, but believe me. Simply live. I have known enough that could not do that.'

The lights of the house glowed in the fog of the narrow horizon.

It was late when West came to Radford's room. He entered without knocking and it took Radford's mind to his old bedroom, his old home. By the end he had come to propping a chair against the handle of the closed door, keeping his room his own and all else outside. Being trapped had been a comfort.

West sat on the end of the bed and spoke as if the time of quiet between them had been unreal. It took Radford some minutes to wake fully but soon they were laughing over the memory of that morning's porridge disaster and how it had befallen Lewis's lap. Someone rapped angrily on a wall.

'Should sleep,' West said and went to leave.

Radford followed, not ready for the easiness to end, feeling no guarantee that it would remain by morning. They were just through the doorway when Lillian shocked them both as she tripped on the stair at the hall's end. A purple robe, the cause of her injury, flapped about her legs. She was already waving them away by the time they reached her.

'Boys, no.' She was distraught and trying to bury its display. 'Back to sleep, go now.' She spoke plainly and beautifully, having abandoned everything French.

'What's the matter?'

'Back to your rooms, please. Please, my darlings.'

'Lill—'

'Darlings.'

She gave up at the sound of Manny shambling up the stairs. 'Lil?' he asked, wanting direction. His face was blushed and stuck with hair.

'Yes, all arranged. The car?'

'Got the engine going now. It will need to warm up.' He covered his mouth, seeing in Lillian's reaction that he had been too loud.

She got in a sudden panic and herded them all upstairs. 'The house will wake. Come, quietly, the three of you.'

They were soon at the top of the stairs and through into Teddy's rooms. Lillian closed the door carefully and set about packing a small suitcase, Manny helping, both seeming oblivious to Teddy's presence. He sat on the bare floor in his pyjamas, his back against the side of his desk, his face down and in his hands.

Radford lingered at the door with West, neither understanding the situation. Teddy did not acknowledge them. He moved only when the suitcase was finished and Lillian said that he was required to dress, taking the bundle of clothes and shoes from her and going behind a screen to change.

His face was the puzzle. It was a look of recent trouble, swollen and dusted with the salt of dried tears, yet showing no engagement of emotion, just its history. The man was somewhere beneath and its eyes had not turned to Radford or West. Teddy was a vapour and his bare feet padded across the floorboards without generating a sound. The dressing screen was a wooden frame around printed fabric: white roses and coral blossoms. They rippled as Teddy finished with his shoes, how flowers would sway under a sweet, tropical breeze.

'Come,' Lillian said and took Teddy out, Manny following with the case. The two men began down the stairs and Lillian returned to the boys. 'Teddy is not well,' she said. 'We have arranged for him to stay in London. You are not to worry. This is something that happens, from time to time, and Teddy will be with good people. Boys? It is not a thing to be concerned with. It will happen, from time to time. Though I will ask a favour of you. My darlings, will you go with Manny? It will make the journey easier for him. Will you dress quickly, now, and go with him?'

They went to their rooms and met again downstairs. They were both in coats when Lillian intercepted West and filled his pockets with wrapped sandwiches. He held two flasks, one tea, the other water. Lillian kissed their cheeks. They jogged out to the car where it waited at the top of the drive, its windows already fogged. They exchanged nods with Manny and the car started off.

The air was free of snow and the road had been recently cleared. Radford took a handkerchief from his pocket and leant through the cabin, wiping the windshield, and he would repeat this motion a hundred times over the course of the drive. Teddy remained immobile in the front passenger seat, all of him covered by the worn red of a blanket.

First light brought the city and with it a reunion more arousing than Radford had prepared for. This place, the only home he should have known, had perished from his memory in the journey with his uncle to the country – he had thought of the city only in fits, when its name was spoken by some newsreader or the other boys. Radford had not pined for London, not a bit, but now, as they entered its northern suburbs, he experienced a rush of pride and then sickness. All was still, disquietingly so. A battlefield dawn. The place had seized, with machines and relics pushed from their places of death to the roadsides, and through their car's vents Radford smelt the exhausted industry.

The sun came above the roofs and began its work on the gloom. Radford lightened and began to sing out street names, first to alert Manny, then because he gloried in this knowledge – in that car he was seer. The sombre mood of night-time lifted, with West sitting forward and Manny taking pleasure in ceding control of their navigation. He dug in his pocket and handed over the slip of paper that Lillian had sent with them. Radford kept them straight on.

He wondered if it was normal to feel unattached to any particular place. He was enjoying this familiarity, but it was only as if he'd found a finger-painting in a box of keepsakes: in the end it would return to the box with the other antiques. They passed parks and an empty, drowned playing field. There was more traffic now and pedestrians strode the footpaths in both directions. They wore coats and hoods but walked with their backs straight, taking the sunlight on their faces. Rubbish was piled high at the street corners.

'Straight on?'

'Keep on.' Radford began to again call street names and he soon had them in the heart of the city. 'Finchley Road, straight on.'

They watched churches and covered lakes slip by. More stern-spined citizens unafraid.

'Will we pass the palace?' West asked.

'We can,' Radford said in the tone of a beneficent father.

West was pleased but Manny asked if they could carry on directly, whichever way would bring them fastest to their destination.

'Of course,' Radford said, at once low with guilt at having to be reminded of their mission.

He allowed himself a glance down at the unflinching mound in the passenger seat. It had remained all the trip a woollen heap. No face or limbs and no sound of a sleeper's heavy breathing to pardon Teddy's absence.

'Sorry, Manny.' West patted his shoulder. 'Of course, whichever way's the quickest.'

They found the place with ease, a numbered house in a quite grand street, a blue door bracketed by columns that stretched up to support the first floor's balcony. Above that were two further storeys of tall, curtained windows.

'This is it.'

'Yes,' Manny said, already unbuckled and getting his door open.

Teddy left the cabin without a word or once turning his head. Radford and West silently queried each other while Manny walked Teddy down the footpath and rang the bell. The door was answered at once by a slight, white-bearded man in a charcoal suit and Teddy was received into the house. The beard stood speaking for only a minute before Manny came back to the car.

'We're leaving?' West asked.

'It's all fine,' Manny said. 'All arranged.'

West pushed forward. 'Will he be okay? I mean, what's happened?'

Manny adjusted the mirror. 'It's all arranged.' He breathed weakly, appealing not to be pushed on the subject.

The boys nodded.

'Shall we have a bit of an outing?' Manny asked, starting the engine. 'While we're here?'

They drove back to the main street and added to the swelling traffic. Radford gave a roll call of destinations, all of which were agreed upon. So a new journey began, the red blanket resting where it had fallen across the front seat.

The three of them endured an entirely pleasant morning, as if the excursion had been planned. They circled as near to the palace as they were able and ditched the car by a bakery, going in for pies, and the baker told them of the Thames freezing over and the trouble with the rubbish and having no salt. Milk was going solid on doorsteps. They took their breakfast in paper bags with buns for later and walked shoulder to shoulder, following the concrete of the river and strolling like honeymooners.

It began to snow, softly, the embers of the lost empire.

They turned inwards for the Square and kept on, starting on their buns as they reached the foot of Nelson's Column. His lions' noses were dressed with snow, which made the three laugh. Buses struggled by with ruthless faces floating behind sheets of glass.

It was growing dark as they approached St James's Park, the temperature plummeting. The palace rose from the edge of the frozen lake: all at its feet was dead and bloodless but a family on skates, cruising and turning at the centre of the ice. The boys rested on a bench and listened to the laughter sailing across the lake. The dimming sunlight recast the dancing as a shadow puppet show.

They watched and Manny told them a story of having to rescue his dog from a lake when he was young. It had followed some ducks across the frozen surface and broken through, clinging on only by its front paws. Manny had laid himself flat and crept along the ice on his toes and fingertips until reaching the dog and dragging it onto his back. It had bitten him hard on the leg and run away for four days.

Manny talked of his time in the war. He then explained that Teddy had, from time to time, difficulties. The beard at the grand house with the blue door was a friend of Teddy's and a doctor. Teddy simply needed a rest, just as anyone, from time to time, needed a rest. He would be back soon and the Manor would continue as before. Manny asked if they could, nevertheless, keep this to themselves and they agreed.

The family skated to the lake's edge, changed into shoes and scurried away. Radford led West and Manny to the far end of the park. Not a single living creature remained in the palace's shadow. The trio took their cue and headed away to find the car as the wind turned ugly and the sky dimmed further still.

*

Lillian's accent failed to return in the days that followed and Teddy's truancy was explained as administrative duty. This inspired precisely the absence of interest desired. Any matters that would usually find their way to Teddy's spire could instead find Lillian in her kitchen.

West had returned to the group but kept at its fringe; they drifted from breakfast to whichever part of the house offered diversion. They ended up in honey-eating piles by the fire or idling an upstairs hall. There were no lessons for the time being – no guests, no new treats. The house erupted into fights more often, which provided flashes of curiosity but nothing sustained. Radford had volunteered as the group's emissary one afternoon to scrounge whatever he was able from the pantries. In the kitchen was Lillian, as he'd hoped.

'No, you will grow fat,' she said. 'It will do you good to grow a little weaker.'

'An orange?'

'Not even a grape.'

'If I go back empty-handed I'll be mangled.'

She went to a drawer and pulled out a short knife, handing it to Radford. 'Here then,' she said. 'Protection.'

He leant into the wall, managing to switch the light off and then on with his shoulder.

'Oh grief, will you leave me be?' She threw him an apple. 'And you've got the knife to cut it so don't any come begging for more.'

He would have returned a grateful smile if he had not in that instant seen Victoria through one of the clouded rear windows. It was her, unmistakably, pacing outside the Manor along a far wall. He looked away from the window too quickly, just as Lillian turned to address West and Brass arriving behind him.

'Out!' She walked at Radford, pushing him into the others and directing them away. 'No more. I have given this one all of your banquet. I do not wish to see you, I do not want to hear you.'

In the hall Radford handed over the fruit and knife. 'I've got to go,' he said, breaking away at the stairs.

'Go where?'

'I don't feel well.'

Radford clutched his stomach and didn't wait for sympathy, leaping to the next floor and waiting with held breath against the top step. When he was sure the others had gone he returned to the kitchen and blurted *firewood* to Lillian as he ran out the back door. He went the opposite direction to where he had sighted Victoria, sure that Lillian would watch through the kitchen glass, then travelled the long way back, ducking between trees. He found Victoria behind the door to the coop, her green coat showing through the knot holes.

'Oh, Radford.'

She came in a deluge of relief and he accepted her in his arms as she fell, all sobbing and laughter. They sat with the chickens. She had been trying the door to Snuffy's old room at the side of the house but had found it secure behind its padlock.

'You must think I'm crazy for being here.'

'The key,' Radford said, standing. 'Wait here.'

The procedure took far too long and every ticking moment seemed to Radford a month. He was made to stop on three separate occasions to conduct three separate, unconvincing conversations – Lillian at her oven, the boy called Rabbit by the toilet, and Lewis, all lithe and unaware of the passing of time. Radford found a chain of likely-looking keys in Teddy's office in the desk's top drawer. His chest stung at the sight of the immaculately made bed with a stack of ironed clothes on its end. Lillian huffed as he escaped again out the kitchen door. He collected Victoria, discovered the right key for Snuffy's place and rushed them inside. Silence fell over them and Victoria walked slowly about, running her finger over objects.

'Do you think we can play a record?' she asked. 'If we keep it very low. Do you think?'

Radford had not thought beyond the instant of escaping into the room. 'I suppose, if it's very quiet.'

She exulted at this and sat herself on the mattress. 'You choose.'

'Victoria, do you really—'

'Please, Radford. Choose.'

This could not end well, he knew that, but he could also not deny the moment's delight. He went to the player and picked a restful-sounding record from the stack, one called *Heavenly*.

'Oh, you know me!' she exclaimed as it came on. 'Snuffy would never play this. Radford, of all the ones.'

She lay down and closed her eyes. He hovered in the centre of the room before going to build the fire. He took from the piles of paper and split wood and made a tent which took light with the first match.

'Have you eaten?' he asked.

It was perhaps ten minutes before she woke and with unopened eyes asked, 'Radford, do you mind if I sleep? You don't mind?'

'I'll need to go,' he said. 'I'll come out as soon as tea's done. I'll bring some food. You stay, stay.'

The room grew sickly warm and Radford drew a chair into the centre. Victoria breathed as safely nested animals did and he turned the record when it needed turning. He left when he was convinced he had listened too long.

It was sticky extracting himself after tea. Rich produced a deck of cards and was intent on getting through several rounds of Commerce, which first involved teaching the thing to Lewis and West. Radford claimed he had no money but West knew this as a lie and called him on it, so he went to his room for coins like the others. They played back by the fire and all the time Radford was worrying horribly over Victoria. The stovepipe might have blocked and she could have choked, dead under the covers. Or this could all have been some rotten business on her part and she was lying with slashed wrists and a note pinned to her front.

Radford reasoned he must win enough hands to warrant excusing himself to protect his earnings. After thirty minutes of only occasional success he switched to a strategy of outright defeat but even this proved difficult thanks to West's pedantry and Lewis's poor memory. Between debate of the relative power of aces over court cards, how a tie in the point was split, and whether the table should be knocked on before or after a player became content with their hand, an hour was gone and Radford had failed to lose even half of his bankroll.

At last Brass deemed it all too dreary and left for a kitchen snoop, which Radford insisted on joining. Brass gave only a grunt when Radford split from him. He had stashed a bowl of stew and two rolls in his room and he went upstairs for these, hiding them inside a folded coat and fleeing through the house's front entrance. He kept to the east wall, crouching as he passed under window frames. He could hear the music from Snuffy's room well before reaching it.

'Victoria, damn it.' He shut the door, put down his bundle and ran to the record player, shutting it off.

'Hey there!' Victoria sang indignantly. 'No, no. I was dancing.'

And she continued to, alone with her bottle of spirits, having undressed to her slip. The room was unbearably hot and he could see that the stove had been crammed to overflowing. Still-glowing pieces of logs had fallen out; the carpet had burnt, leaving a singed halo.

'Dance with me,' she said and reached out. 'Please.'

'You've nearly set the place alight.'

'Don't be cross.'

He attempted to read her but could see nothing behind the gloss of drunkenness. Her skin was wet and the sweat dripped from her nose and fingers as she began to slowly spin.

'I was a ballerina,' she said, rising to the toes of her bare feet. 'Did I say? When I was young.'

'There's food here when you're hungry.'

He pointed to his coat and after a time, realising that her attention was beyond him, moved to the mattress and sat against the wall. She rushed over and handed him the bottle.

'Here, take this. It's making me sick.'

This couldn't last, any of it. They would be found out; it was only a question of when and whether it would be the fault of the smoke or noise or Radford's absence. He took a drink and was pleased by his tolerance for its bite. He crept to the record player and started its music again, quieter, then returned to the mattress. The brickwork was hot against his shoulders.

'Why have you come?' he asked.

She became still, her eyes full with intent. 'I wasn't sure, but it's obvious. So obvious. We must run away together. Oh please!'

'Victoria—'

'You never did that when you were young? It will be just the same, but we won't head back when we reach the end of the street. Let's pack a case and go to the city. We're the same. We will figure it all out – we'll be such friends, I'll find work, we'll get a flat. You know we're the same. Please, Radford, answer without thinking. Will you come?'

Words came naturally despite the question's surprise. 'I can't.'

'You won't.'

'That's right, I won't.'

Victoria took in two deep breaths, exhaling each through firmed lips. To Radford, the idea hid no obvious fault, yet he was denying it. To go with her would be all life's adventures in one. But he would not. His feet were rooted to the floor because to go with her would be leaving home. The idea was a new and fearful one and he felt such pride in its discovery.

There was the unbearable thought of Teddy returning to find him gone. There was friendship. There was West.

She eased and began to pivot at her hips. 'For the best. I'd only tire of you.'

'No doubt.'

Their eye-lines locked and the present corrected itself peacefully into the past.

'I've remembered something. Are you watching?' she said.

'Fouetté.'

Rising again she began to turn. With each revolution she would whip her working leg out and then tuck it behind the knee of the other. The music beat out of time, failing to match her. Victoria fought her forgetful body, winning, keeping straight like a pin with her chin raised and disciplined. Her smile grew.

'Come eat,' he said.

She planted her feet, swung her arm down, bowing to Radford's applause, and came crookedly over to sit. She fell hard against his hip and looked unwell. She slapped away the whisky in his hand.

'Yuck, that's made me sick.'

'Here.'

She ate like the meal was her first or last, using a bread roll as cutlery and leaving smears of gravy across her face. When she was finished she cleaned her face with a corner of the bedsheet and sighed with contentment, then went quiet. Radford let her lie against his arm though it brought pins and needles. The fire was calming but with Victoria on him the heat was too great and sweat ran across his brow and stung his eyes.

'Don't know why,' she said.

'What's that?'

'Why I've come. Don't know why.'

He wished he could offer her comfort, to give her any of what he had found.

She brought two fingers to her temple. 'It was great fun to dance again. Maybe that's why. I'd forgotten all about it, that I was a ballerina. I was, you know, I'm not making it up.'

'I saw.'

'When I was a little thing I danced all over the place. Then I gave up. Got bored with it, I suppose. That's silly, isn't it? Something you do when you're a little one – get bored with things.'

They sat for a long time in their congested peace. They both dipped into half-sleep, both took whisky.

'Radford, how did you end up being sent here?'

He straightened his hair and sipped again from the drink. 'We don't tell,' he said. 'We don't tell that, unless we want to.'

'And you don't want to? God, Snuffy would never stop with the stories of all the things he did to end up here. And what he did to keep being sent back.'

Radford laughed and settled, feeling for her weight against him.

'Will you show me again?' he asked. 'Your ballet.'

'Only if you dance with me.'

He thought of what that would be like. He imagined their touching then was interrupted by the memory of West and Foster and their cruelty beneath the trees. He thought of the other times, in his old home, before coming to the new. Victoria's hand was still outstretched in invitation.

'No,' he said. 'Just you.'

'Okay.' She put her hands again to her temples. 'Did you know this was a wig?' As she shoved her fingers under her hairline they disappeared beyond the nails. 'I thought Snuffy might have told you.'

In the room's middle she began to circle around, pointing her toes and bringing up her chest. In a motion as serene she went on pushing her fingers under her hair and ran them back and around, until all of the wig came away and she dropped it to the ground, a dull hat. She closed her eyes, showing relief, and let the pads of her fingers run across her bald scalp. The crest of her head reflected the vaporous orange of the single hanging bulb, and she danced.

The movements were as before but now she radiated in the way that bonfires burnt. Yellow smoke could well have poured from her hands as she spun and spun, putting to hell all the refuse and wasted things that the season had accumulated. Radford recalled being drawn to bonfires when he was young and of dogs being frightened away. He saw only the fire's ecstatic power, that it bowed to no authority, while the animals perhaps knew that the demon could steal a whole body without being seen, only to be noticed in the morning as the ashes were raked. Victoria danced and Radford thought it all the more perfect for knowing that like the fire it could not go on forever. It was a fleeting, almighty thing and he would not disturb it as it charged on and on through its supplies. She was a ballerina and he was her audience; he applauded and she accepted.

Eventually Victoria grew tired and they sat together.

'I'll just stay a night,' she said. 'I'll steal away in the morning. Don't want to cause trouble.'

'No, stay, as long as you need. I'll talk to Lillian. When the time comes Manny and I will drive you to the city. Stay.'

She agreed and slept, but in the morning when he came to the room before breakfast he found the mattress empty and made. She had gone, leaving no note or clue. The fire was out and the player's needle travelled within the record's run-out groove, exploring endlessly.

*

They waited on Teddy's return. It had been a week and Radford and West said nothing on the matter. Silence here, Radford concluded, was the truest act of loyalty.

The others, though, had begun to question his absence. It was during such an afternoon conference by the fire that Radford sought to put a short in the subject. All the close crew were there. Brass yawned. Lewis proposed some theory. Rich was in a generous mood and was attacking all with wads of chewed-up newspaper.

'Who's for the graveyard?' Radford asked when it seemed that Lewis would never tire and Rich would find no end to ammunition.

'Surely not again?' Lewis said. 'Too far. Too cold.'

'I've grog,' Radford said.

While finding his coat Radford worried that Victoria would not have left enough to legitimise the excursion but when he led the troupe outside and ducked to Snuffy's room he found a third of the whisky remained. He returned to the tree shadows and they celebrated.

The same words, all the same, over and over – yet in the tedium there was now solace.

They marched out of the grounds with no concern of being seen. Lillian would object but not to any real degree and Manny would raise no complaint. So they passed between the ruins of the end wall and into the unprotected world, and as they went all except West fell into customary pairings and battles. He stayed a stride's length behind Radford, who twice tried to slow. At each attempt the line of West's shoulders would remain that steady yard in the past.

The cemetery gave itself away only by the very tips of a short dozen headstones and the two taller monuments now reduced to waist height. The perimeter railing was beneath pale ground though it was found by the underside of Lewis's foot. He claimed one of its barbs had pierced his boot and Rich's pretended sympathy came on strong, ending with them rolling about until Lewis struck his head against one of the ancient slabs.

They milled around making space in front of stones so that they could sit. The drink went around and each took modest sips. When it came to Radford the whisky aroused a vision of Victoria, and that in turn made him stare upwards into the afternoon to give an excuse to his watering eyes. He brought the neck to his lips a second time and made all the motions that were customary but stopped the flow of booze with his tongue. West showed no such modesty and the bottle gave up its contents in a messy, blubbing show; it was only the shouting of the others that brought it to a stop.

'Jesus, go easy,' Brass demanded.

West dropped the bottle at his feet, burying it in the ground. 'Jesus, yes. You've uncovered my secret, I'm the Son of God!' West said, going wild. 'After all this time.' He cast himself backwards and hard against a low stone cross.

'Oh look,' Brass said. 'He's gone all *theatre*.'

'No, quite the opposite. I've gone truthful at last. I'm dead, don't you see?'

Nobody answered but Radford walked towards him, putting a hand out. Brass turned away and finished the last of the drink. The others looked to Radford as if he might know what part of this was the joke.

'The wake,' West began. 'It must begin. Ahem. West – he was a decent boy.'

Brass continued what was to be a slow walk, hands in pockets, to the far side of the cemetery.

'Decent, yes,' West continued. 'Though not without fault. Ask the mother – though the mother of mankind's saviour is going to end up let down, isn't she?'

Radford asked him to stop.

'And the father? Well, he kept his customary distance. Very *hands-off*, isn't he? For the planter of the holy seed. But no, I've trailed off the point,' West went on. 'How did West die? Let's say it was in the usual way. The usual, inevitable way.'

'That's enough,' Radford said, this time finding force and taking West's hand rather than waiting for it.

They all remained silent for some time, West alone smiling. The drink was gone and the break in weather seemed without purpose. All flames had been snubbed, all close to being lost.

'Have you seen the starlings?' Radford asked abruptly.

Out they came again to Winter, muddying its carpet. All they seemed to want was to tease with their actions. If only they were to declare themselves, to show their colours. So little was wanted from them, just a handshake, some understanding.

Winter would send all its weary messengers. Every last animal would soon have to decide – it could not go on in this way.

The boys stood in wonder, for above them the sky was breaking apart. It seemed to Radford exactly how a mirage might present itself. The starlings had lifted from their roost and swarmed into a molten object which oscillated above the horizon, making impossible shapes. They were a snake, a heart, a firework. The flock breathed with a lone purpose and it was this unity that struck him. That all these beaks and breakable wings could come so close to disaster yet make a song so sweet. It made its way into his pulse, rising and falling as the colony moved closer or away.

'Seen this before?' he said as the formation turned into a long arrowhead and aimed itself at the setting sun.

There were a few shaking heads.

'Mad.' Rich looked to Lewis.

'Mad.'

'I've seen it,' West said. His voice had softened. 'Years ago with my parents in Devon. My father used to take us with his caravan to Slapton Ley and we'd go for these awful walks.'

'What is it?'

'It's called a murmuration.' West ran his hands through his hair. 'A man at the park told us. I haven't thought of that word since I was eight. I made him spell it out – how on earth has that stayed in my head?'

They stood as silhouettes in the silver distance and the birds continued unaware. Radford knew it was no scheduled performance, just a happening of instinct. He put his arm over West's shoulder and it was not shrugged away. The birds did not collide, nor were they led hopeless into the ground, yet their flight took place as if under a leader's direction. They were just getting by and that was some good spell.

They stayed until the light failed. The flock separated in a sudden gesture and they were once again mere birds in trees. As the boys made their way back Rich was the first to notice blood. Starling bodies lay across the snow as Radford had seen with Teddy but now others had come to some sicker end: their bodies had been maimed and the dark blood beneath formed uneven streaks. The cold hadn't done this.

West took one carefully in his hands. 'What has happened to you?'

The other boys stood around and peered in. Lewis pulled at West's sleeve.

'Some animal,' Brass said.

West continued to stare into the thing while the others began to fidget. The wind rose and made sharp to Radford their exposure. They were right to be afraid.

'Come on, we'll be stuck,' Lewis said with a measure of urgency.

They moved away in the direction of home and nothing more was said. They made quick time to the house despite the dark and when they came into the dining room they found Teddy eating soup by the fire.

After tea Radford came upon Lillian in her kitchen, a cigarette at her lips. He went for an apple from the basket.

'Come here,' she said and placed him by her side, digging in with her hip.

'It's just an apple.'

She took a cigarette from her bib and gave it to Radford. He waited as she struck a match and the two of them insisted on quiet, the only sound the hustle of air between them.

'Teddy's back,' Radford said.

'Correct.'

They continued puffing and when another boy appeared in the doorway Lillian snarled at him until he left. She stubbed out against the basin.

'Thank you, my son. What you did for Teddy, your help.'

'Please, no.'

He read forgiveness in her face.

'You help,' she said and silenced his disapprovals. 'I see it. I witness all in this house and I see you help West. You help

Teddy. This is a kind thing you do.'

'I don't do a thing, Lillian.'

'You are there.' She held his wrist. 'That is no small affair. You stay. It is not as common as you must think. And it is Lil, please, my love.'

She brought him close and he shut his eyes, falling into a standing dream. She stroked his ear, his brow. She ran her fingers through his hair until he lost all feeling.

EIGHT

The thaw arrived with no apology. One morning warmth was simply present where the day before cold had been, and the earth creaked at its presence. The trees swayed a groom's dance and shook their snow. Infinite tiny rivulets formed from the melting ice while the Manor listened to its radios and had confirmed what was plain fact out its windows. The Big Freeze was over. It had left only mud, its tracks obscured, and, with each passing day of that first thaw week, only more mud. Lil grew crazy with it being dragged through the house while Teddy took the assault as a playful thing. He roused the boys to scrub the slush from the floors while ensuring its return by sending troops out to make overdue repairs and to help with Gall and his fields. In the champagne of the new season Teddy was showing every sign of life.

Radford was with the others before tea when the announcement came on the news: it was the first morning of the year without reports of frost from any corner of Britain. Teddy came in rubbing his hands, delighted, and commanded West to the piano. The curtains were pulled back, the midday light remembered its task and West obliged with 'When I'm Cleaning Windows'. As the food arrived everyone was singing, even the sports boys. Radford stood on the long table with Lewis and led the chant while Lil screamed about the boots but sang along all the same. West came back to his seat and wore a look of tired pride, becoming unusually talkative. He pushed around the dishes of bread and butter and made it his job to serve the minced beef and boiled potatoes. Teddy decreed that they should enjoy this last leisured afternoon as from the next morning they would be going into the village to help with the clean-up. They would be an army and it would be a term of action like they had never known. The forgotten thing, spring. He continued to rub his hands.

At the wall ruins Radford stood with Teddy as dusk came. He felt some vacant pity for the Freeze's demise, knowing it could not hold on to the evidence of its existence for long. The hills would rise as a green shadow, piercing through at their peaks and swallowing the winter's remains.

 West had gone ahead and was at the boundary of the next hill, walking across the top of its stone wall. He did this with no purpose, just skipping from flat to flat, and Radford and Teddy stopped to watch with as little aim. Manny was digging out the chicken coop behind them.

 'Did anyone tell you about the starlings?' Radford asked. 'We saw them flying around in a, what's it called? Like a cloud.'

 'Wish I'd been there.' Teddy kept his eyes on West, raising a hand to shield them from the sun. 'You know why I was away?'

Radford would continue to be truthful. 'Yes. I think so.'

'Is there anything you'd like to ask?'

A bird flew low over his shoulder, startling him. The creature went on untroubled. 'I'm not sure, Teddy. I'd like to know about it, and you can tell me if you like, but is that ... best?'

He laughed. 'I'm not certain I know. Still, I would like to tell you.'

'Yes, then.'

'I have a trouble that finds me often enough. When it's too much to bear I go to stay in a place that's helpful. This time it was the house in the city, where you left me. It really is quite straightforward. I'm treated as an invalid for a few days and some strength returns and I'm treated like a child. I talk for a time with my friend and when I begin to be treated as an adult it's time for me to be sent home. It's merely something that happens.' Teddy turned away from the glare. 'It is nothing to be ashamed of and I share this with my dear ones.'

'Yes.'

They watched West bound against the pearl. 'It is a great thing, to know what is yours,' Teddy said. 'This is mine to tell.'

The breeze that ran over them was almost lovely.

'That first night,' Radford said. 'The first night I was here. I was going to throw myself out of the belfry window. Or some other solution, something as effective.'

'Yes.'

'I didn't though, of course. And I won't. As far as a promise like that can see into the future, I promise you I won't.'

'Then, as far into the future as that lasts, thank you.' Teddy said. 'Pointless, aren't they? Promises.'

'I've always thought so.'

Their laughter synchronised.

'What day is it?' Teddy asked.

'Sunday.'

'Oh right, that makes sense.'

Radford wondered if his answer had been true. He had never taken to Sundays in the way that others leapt at it. It was that day that should be rest, would be a holiday, if it wasn't always poisoned with the promise of what came after. Not that Mondays ever really came. It was always that everlasting Sunday, the unending anticipation.

One decent winter survived and here he was, thinking himself profound. Radford laughed aloud at his philosophy.

'The newspaper says it was the coldest season in three hundred years,' Teddy said.

'That makes sense.'

A second bird buzzed by Radford as it fired from the Manor grounds and ahead. He considered if they were all in fact in love with the cold, and now all would be exposed and all would be real. There would be no more excuses, and that thought terrified. The bird disappeared as it went straight for the shape of West, who in turn disappeared into the contour of the hill. Perhaps the thaw would take care of all this, one way or the other. Everything would fall away. The house, its people, the sky and its birds, all tumbling with the other remnants into the valley.

That night Radford woke in fright as if a book had closed beside his ear and he lay in the darkness for some time examining his dimming memories. He tried to draw a line between events, seeking a trajectory that made sense and would leave them in a configuration he could be comfortable with. Failing at this he dressed, checking his clock by the window light, and went softly into the hall. He would take West for a midnight smoke, and they would talk if he wished it, and it would repair a little the tear that seemed to have formed in his friend. *His friend*. Radford warmed and steeled himself by those words.

West was not in his room and the journey downstairs was colourless though well lit. The excitement of the thaw had overtaken reason and throughout the house every curtain had been thrown open, despite the night. Full moonlight came in, showing all that was not. West would be in the kitchen scavenging or in the dining room devouring and that would be a welcome sign despite the sleeplessness.

So many questions rolled about Radford's mind, colliding with one another. He wondered when exactly he had become brother to West's comfort and whether it happened through sheer proximity and familiarity or only by the sharing of trouble. If love came on the back of violence then perhaps that was not love but fear. But fear was wanting not to be without, and that could be all love was, in truth. What was wrong with being scared? Or being thick or angry or hopeless. He would discuss all these things with West and they would come to conclusions.

Reaching the kitchen he discovered Lewis on hands and knees up against the frame of the pantry door. He was hovering above one of the mousetraps, inching down towards it with a dirty rolled towel. Radford held his breath. The trap was sprung and its hammer came down powerfully but almost silently against the fabric. Radford watched on as Lewis moved from trap to trap, disarming each in turn. So this had been the vermin's salvation.

Radford stepped past the dining room, where a figure occupied the reading chair: he saw by the meagre firelight that it was Teddy. A book was open in his lap but his attention was on only his pipe as he chewed on its bit. No glow or smoke came from the pipe's chamber and Teddy believed himself alone. Radford knew Teddy would hate the thought, but he wanted nothing but to find a course through life that would lead him to this place. It did not matter that Teddy was subject to weakness, that he possessed within him a vein of painful blood and that he spent midnights by a failing fire, chomping on his pipe. He was alive and had others to care for and this was enough to hope for.

Radford backed away as quickly as he dared and returned to the kitchen, now empty. That moon came through the freshly washed windows and fell on a dish of green apples resting beneath a muslin cloth. He saw the door leading outside was ajar. It let out a dull creak as it opened under the power of a wind that ruffled Radford's hair. He checked his coat and went outside. West would be smoking around one of the Manor's corners. Radford would find him and convince him up to their belfry, where time could still be made to run slower and they could begin the rebuilding of their thrones.

The gun was leaning against the trunk of a tree in such clear sight, in a way that seemed so natural, that Radford wasn't startled. He picked it up as if collecting wood for the fire, but when he felt its weight and looked down its barrel to the grey earth a tremble ran through the grain of his muscles.

It was a shotgun and it could only have been Farmer Gall's. For a moment it felt right in Radford's possession – he forgot his confusion and revelled in the excitement of wielding this antiquated, all-powerful thing. He could make war. A king could be liberated to history with a single action. The cowboy games he played as a younger boy seemed now to have been training for this. He smiled at the thought and walked on, only then giving full thought to how this object could have ended up on the house grounds. The trigger guard brushed the blade of his finger.

He and Foster saw each other in the same instant and both were possessed by an equal measure of alarm. Foster stood from where he had been crouching at the foot of an ivory tree. Radford continued forward, raising the shotgun level by childish instinct.

'Hello,' Radford said flatly. 'What's there—'

Foster turned into the light and his whole front was covered in blood. Radford knew it could be nothing else, up the creature's arms, across his chest, against the flesh of his neck. Foster held out a knife and the blade was dark and shone wet.

'I know he told you.' Foster spoke in a brittle tone.

'What have you done?'

Radford continued to repeat this question, quieter each time, knowing the answer. On the ground behind Foster, reclined against the tree, was West, cut to pieces. His shirt had been torn from his body, leaving a chest that was all wounds and horror. The skin of his face was already pale beyond possibility; his features made no boundary with the earth.

'I know he told,' Foster said. 'He had no right.' He was growing brave now, standing at full height, his face twisting into aggression. 'There were two of us in this.'

Radford thought only of the cold. How it would be burning West's skin if he could feel it. Winter was slipping underground, taking with it its trouble. He understood what it had all been for.

Foster raged with all his untrue evil, raising the knife at Radford's neck, lunging, coming at once to join him in the tree's shadow. West could no longer speak and so neither would Radford. He instead kept the gun steady and pulled the trigger like he had done a thousand times as a playing boy and watched as its shot tore Foster apart. The animal's body was flung backwards, landing soft among the slush and litter. The knife lay beside its open palm. Radford remained, his ears disabled by the blast and with the force of the gun's recoil aching through his shoulder and chest. As if from a distance he saw himself doubled in the deserting snow. There was nothing to do. Nothing could happen now and so no action could have consequence. He stood in place and watched West return, beautiful and absolute, through the descending mist of pink.

Some quantity of time transpired before Teddy came from behind and snatched the shotgun. He spoke frantically and Radford could make no sense of it. Teddy knelt beside the bodies, first Foster's and then West's. He stood and held Radford at his throat, shaking him and shouting furious questions.

Radford explained.

Teddy was briefly silent before describing what was to happen. Radford was to forget all he thought he remembered of this. A series of linear events had taken place: Radford had been in the kitchen seeking supper when he heard the shot; he had run out to the grounds and come across this scene of two boys painted red and Teddy standing above them with the gun; Teddy had offered no reason for the spectacle and shouted at him to return inside. This was what had occurred – this, and only this. Radford was made to say that he understood.

Teddy turned away with the weapon. 'So then, back to the house.'

These were the unremarkable words that Radford would remember. Such plain and fatherly sentiments, spoken so mildly. He would recall many things but it was this message of Teddy's that would remain most clearly. *So then, back to the house.*

When Radford reached the kitchen he was met by boys coming the other way, ignoring him and rushing outside in search of the drama. Others would pass through the kitchen. Brass, Rich, Lewis. Lil and Manny too. All of the house, in time. There was screaming and tears. Talk and talk about causes. Mostly wrong, all so terrible. Radford corrected no-one. Through all that followed he would correct not one of the lies told by Teddy. His role was reduced to inconsequence, as Teddy had described, as he had agreed to.

Foster and West's true story, whatever it had been, was lost. What past they shared – the mechanics of its destruction.

Radford knew it in parts but still insufficiently. Two halves joined and yet whatever fullness they made had been taken with them.

Winter watched strangers come to the house and their arrival marked its final silence. There was no learning to be done. No message. It had come and done its work and for this coldest boy there would be no last words.

Radford had lost his chance to ask his friend questions on the likeness of fear and love and violence, so in the time that followed he built a conclusion of his own and settled on following the path it described. Whether it would exist in reality as it did in promise, he concluded it was as perfect a plan as any other.

If Winter had lingered he would have shared with it his new belief.

But, now, he was alone.

That night he stood by the cold ovens watching the moon descend on trouble. He watched it come uninvited through the windows, to fall on the dish of shrouded green apples.

NINE

It was a little after midnight on a Sunday, a handful of weeks before the child Radford would be sent to the Manor. He could, naturally, appreciate nothing of that then. All he knew was the sensation of the carpet of his parents' bedroom against his feet. The rest of the house was all floorboards and thin rug. This was rare, sacred ground.

Later, during his single season at the Manor, over its eternal nights, he would remember the thread of his parents' carpet more sharply than any of the events that it preceded: his mother's screams, his uncle and the police being called; the sobbing and accusations; his father, still alive and recovered as far as he would ever be, having to be restrained from apocalyptic revenge.

Radford knew only the carpet under his toes as he stood over his sleeping parents and, perhaps distantly, the feel of the old leather belt taut between his hands. His lone thought in that final act, and it wasn't a thought that sat heavily in his mind: *why don't more sons kill their fathers?*

TEN

The Indian watched a vulture flying high above a rabbit, so *I* equalled *V* over *R*. Radford found himself rehearsing this as he drove by the suburbs of London.

The motorway came to a standstill outside Heathrow and he took pleasure in this. He secretly longed for jams, red lights, anything that meant he could relax his attention from clutches and changing lanes. Driving never became that great conductor of freedom that the commercials guaranteed. For Radford, that job was fulfilled by daydreaming, something that was occupying more and more of what should have been his waking hours, and he was content with this. The lanes started up and he joined the crawl north-west, checking the address again from the open notebook on the seat of the passenger side. Beside this was a folded map with the destination marked with a cross. It would be maybe an hour and a half to Oxford from here, longer if he stopped at a bakery as he planned to.

The day was forecast to be wonderfully midsummer and he had brought along a book to read in sight of the Camera, as dopey and tourist-like as such an activity might be, but that was to be after. He had a pencil for sketching, though in his heart he knew it would remain mint. This was all in aid of a trick, to convince himself that the journey was a minor one. A Saturday of leisure, visiting an acquaintance the way typical people visited their typical acquaintances.

He could picture the vulture circling the scorched plain, so *I* surely still equalled *V* over *R*.

The traffic was flowing smoothly now and Radford had to remind himself to lower his foot on the accelerator. A small convoy had banked up in his rear-view mirror: he deployed his apology wave and reluctantly brought his Marina up to the limit and heard its reliable parts hum their moving song.

The village, like all but the truly remote, had come to resemble all the others, with their identical supermarkets and newsagents. There seemed to be a betting shop for every last man, woman and child. Radford finished these unoriginal thoughts. He'd been doing more of that lately: autopilot thinking that drifted towards crankiness. He was determined to keep the habit in check, it being the horse that perpetually grumpy middle-age rode in on.

He turned off the car's radio, thinking its noise might be replaced by some pastoral hymn, but rising in its place was only the chorus of tyres on bitumen. He played at the gold ring hanging by its chain around his neck.

The house was a couple of miles outside the town centre. Its cream pebble brought a satisfying sound as Radford parked. He had cross-checked his notebook's address with the letterbox number and made the decision to pull in, rather than stop a more cautious distance up the street. This was intended to mean he couldn't sit idly at the wheel pondering the wisdom of the excursion but, having arrived in plain view, sit and ponder he did. Several minutes passed and he remained in his seat. It was a sweet, overgrown house. Ivy scaled its walls, closing in around the windows and climbing onto the lip of its steep slate roof. The lawn was spotted with delicate yellow flowers. Radford reached into one of his brown paper bags and found an iced bun. He had purchased too much from the bakery. He would eat the bun and go in: this was acceptable, he told himself. The sugar would focus his mind, fuel conversation.

Two loud raps on the window caused him to jump and choke.

It was Teddy at the car door, his face smiling an inch from the glass. 'Coming in?'

They sat in the conservatory making unproductive attempts at the great riches of food. Teddy had baked biscuits, scones, lemon tarts and an apple cake. He had Radford carry in a third small table from the next room to accommodate the addition of the bakery parcels.

They talked of small things and Teddy pushed open the glass doors. Behind was a garden consisting of a narrow path cutting through a profusion of sunflowers. They stood as a peaceful army, well above the height of the old man who had gone out to join them with his arms stretched high, all pulsing blonde. The path led to a small clearing with a sundial atop a stone plinth, and beyond that a young, plush oak occupying the far corner. When the tree was grown, Teddy explained, it would flood the garden with shade and cast the sundial into retirement.

'They've come well this year,' he said as they returned inside, flicking his hand in the direction of the flowers. 'Was the mildness of the season just gone.'

Daylight was toasting the earth into scent. All was honey on grass and split cinnamon, and Radford found himself speaking more easily. He was a grown man and so, he reasoned, it should not be difficult to speak to another of his kind. Teddy's age was still impossible to gauge and now seemed irrelevant. The two most recent decades – Radford recoiled at the idea that his memories could be measured in decades – had blunted Teddy's voice but not his gaze. It had been twenty full years since the two of them had spoken. Slightly less than that since Radford had seen the photographs of Teddy in the newspapers. The attention had been fevered for a time, though abandoned once the truth of the matter was decided on. In the pictures Teddy had seemed alone with his fate.

'Lou would rather I rip up the sunflowers and let her have her country garden,' Teddy said, sitting for the third time. 'Cornflowers and roses, and an old fogey's bench. It will happen eventually, of course, but I'll hang on as long as I can.'

'Lou?'

'Louise, my wife.'

'Teddy, I didn't know. Congratulations.'

'Some time ago now. Wedding was, ah, that summer of '76. Yes, '76.'

They toasted their apple juices and looked out as a bee made its way across the garden. It would hover at the flowers' feast, burrowing its head briefly before skirting to the next, devoid of competition.

'How are you?' Teddy asked.

'Not married.'

They looked into each other and laughed.

'No,' Teddy said, 'but you have people?'

Radford came forward in his seat and rested his elbows on his knees. His smile was falling though he felt no sadness. 'Of course,' he said.

'Friends? Good friends?'

'Teddy, yes, of course I do.'

'Good.' Teddy's face reflected a little of the colour from his flowers. 'Good. That is all I hoped.'

'That's about all I have though,' Radford said.

'If you have that, you have a lot.'

They toasted, again, to their unremarkable fragility, and a breeze ran through the house.

'And you, Teddy?'

'Not as many as I might like.' They chuckled, though with less gusto. 'But some, yes. And Lou, of course.'

Teddy put his hands together and placed them between Radford's palms. He closed his fingers around Teddy's hands and they sat like this, embraced again, for some stretch of time. Teddy began to speak, just as Radford noticed the small button of tears that had formed in the folds of the old man's eyes.

'Boy, I've done you wrong.'

At once Radford wanted to voice his disagreement, but he kept his mouth shut. This was not the time and he was perhaps not even the one to make the point. He had, after all, promised to remain silent.

'I've done wrong by giving you this burden. That's how I've come to see it,' Teddy said. 'I can only say I believed I was doing the best by you, truly. If I'd left you there, I can only imagine how things would have gone. I've thought about it all so much and I'm left only with the hope that it all would have been much worse. It's a selfish conclusion but we invent ways to get by, don't we?'

Radford kept his grip.

'Time was I would pray for your forgiveness,' Teddy said. 'And then I'd pray it never came and you would live all your years gloriously in spite of me.'

The bee had come inside now and was bothering the apple cake. Teddy smiled hard as his tears came down.

'The house was to be a brief truce,' he said. 'I knew what had come before, for you all, and I suspected what was to come after. It was just to be some little peace, that you might carry with you. Good grief, I'm saying too much and too little. All this time and I'm still unprepared – you'd think I would've rehearsed.'

Radford watched the anarchy of the bee, wondering what it must think of all the sweetness before it.

'There was a very real way I let you down.' Teddy rubbed at his watering eyes. 'I had the menial task of keeping you all alive and in the end the failure came by my own hand. I care less that the Manor was dismantled. That was merely a great shame and I have not earnt the right of being sentimental.'

A little age had brought Radford opinions, and not only the ones on supermarkets and betting shops. He had come to some conclusions on the workings of history, that time could turn some memories solid in the same slow way wood petrified. Others it would make brittle and they would go to dust. The house stood.

From the direction of town a bell tolled and they paused at its sound, their hands releasing. It seemed a sign to stand and they moved outside.

'Funeral, at the church,' Teddy said patiently.

The brass song floated towards the hills and its distant colony of birds. Perhaps they would be jealous when they heard it, of what graceful thing could make that note. Radford was smiling. He made a face of such pleasure that it would have appeared he was in agony.

There would be no daydreams of changing weather, of rest, of returning home. Instead – unprompted, in sunshine – he thought of West. For the first time in many years he forced himself to remember in detail and was surprised that this brought with it no pain. He had known so little of the boy, this was the truth of it. Though he did know the kindness of a friend and how it had sustained him. That this was all that could truly sustain.

Fragments returned, kid voices:

So what's the point?

Who promised you a point?

The path set out by the Manor was a dangerous one, but all ways were dangerous and at least its way demanded it was not taken alone. Much had occurred since those days. A life,

Radford trusted. He had held and released the hands of many others. Yet after everything that came, it was still that winter of the Manor that illustrated him most truthfully, for it was incomplete.

'You made other promises, you forget,' Radford said and straightened Teddy's stuck collar, giving a soldierly bump on the shoulder. 'Ones as great as keeping us alive. You told me that you weren't to be our friend. Yes? So it would be a failure if you and I were to be friends?'

Radford inhaled from the candied atmosphere and stepped back inside, beginning work at the largest wedge of cake. From the front of the house came the sound of keys and the door unlocking.

The old man nodded.

'Then yes,' Radford said, offering to cut a piece for Teddy. 'In that alone we are agreed. You have failed. Failed miserably.'

A companion to the memory of West arrived, the question of that winter of their youth having abandoned them so abruptly. In time he had come to accept its wordless departure as disapproval, but now, facing the sunflowers and their mild earth, he remembered the depth of cold that was possible in his bones. It now seemed so obvious. The great cold had left no message at their parting for it had never left him.

All that was shaded and hurtful had been silenced. A path made itself clear, one that ran ahead recklessly, seeking company ahead of certainty. The light directed to such obvious things, to friendship and its protection. One had people and so one had duties and this was a miraculous thing.

It was the conclusion of a child, but then we are forever children.

They shared this final secret as someone came into the kitchen. She deposited bags on the counter and continued through to the conservatory, where she introduced herself as Louise and stood behind Teddy, her hands all love around the trunk of his neck.

'So, what have you boys been gossiping about?' She planted a kiss on Teddy's bald crown.

The old man smiled now and Radford turned to the flowers and rejoiced. At trouble unfixed. At Winter's return and the ringing of a bell.